Messenger

Also by Carol Lynch Williams

Glimpse
Waiting
Signed, Skye Harper

Messenger

Carol Lynch Williams

A Paula Wiseman Book

Simon & Schuster Books for Young Readers

NEW YORK   LONDON   TORONTO   SYDNEY   NEW DELHI

SIMON & SCHUSTER BOOKS FOR YOUNG READERS

An imprint of Simon & Schuster Children's Publishing Division

1230 Avenue of the Americas, New York, New York 10020

This book is a work of fiction. Any references to historical events, real people, or real places are used fictitiously. Other names, characters, places, and events are products of the author's imagination, and any resemblance to actual events or places or persons, living or dead, is entirely coincidental.

Text copyright © 2016 by Carol Lynch Williams

Jacket photographs copyright © 2016 by Lumina Images/Getty Images and Victoria Avvacumova/Getty Images

All rights reserved, including the right of reproduction in whole or in part in any form.

SIMON & SCHUSTER BOOKS FOR YOUNG READERS

is a trademark of Simon & Schuster, Inc.

For information about special discounts for bulk purchases, please contact Simon & Schuster Special Sales at 1-866-506-1949 or business@simonandschuster.com.

The Simon & Schuster Speakers Bureau can bring authors to your live event. For more information or to book an event, contact the Simon & Schuster Speakers Bureau at 1-866-248-3049 or visit our website at www.simonspeakers.com.

Jacket design by Chloë Foglia

Interior design by Hilary Zarycky

The text for this book was set in Bodoni.

Manufactured in the United States of America

First Edition

10 9 8 7 6 5 4 3 2 1

Library of Congress Cataloging-in-Publication Data

Names: Williams, Carol Lynch, author.

Title: Messenger / Carol Lynch Williams.

Description: First Edition. | New York : Simon & Schuster Books for Young Readers, [2016] | "A Paula Wiseman Book." | Summary: "Evie Messenger, who can see and talk to ghosts, tries to solve the mystery of a teenage ghost who is following her"—Provided by publisher.

Identifiers: LCCN 2015049285| ISBN 9781481457767 (hardback) | ISBN 9781481457781 (eBook)

Subjects: | CYAC: Ghosts—Fiction. | Ability—Fiction. | Supernatural—Fiction. | Mystery and detective stories. | BISAC: JUVENILE FICTION / Family / General (see also headings under Social Issues). | JUVENILE FICTION / Love & Romance.

Classification: LCC PZ7.W65588 Ev 2016 | DDC [Fic]—dc23

LC record available at https://lccn.loc.gov/2015049285

For my very own Momma—
and all her nine aunts and uncles

Messenger

At first I'm sure someone peers at me. Leans close to my face. Her hair (yes, it's a girl) brushes against my cheek. Her fingers on my shoulder. A close inspection of my room and then right back to where I'm lying. Checking.

A wail pushes through a wall, cries in the night, squeezes at my heart.

She moves toward the sound. Comes back to me. Watches. Swims through the darkness. Disappears. Reappears. Like the anguish pulls her. Like moving to a dance. Or the waves of the ocean.

1

The Gift.

Fifteen.

Fifteen.

I awoke with a gasp, sitting straight up.

Aunt Odie sat in the rocker Momma used to sit in (and rock me) after I was born. Where Momma sat for a bit after Baby Lucy was born (before she bought my sister her own rocker to take with her later on down the road, when *she* grows up some). Momma's a planner.

My aunt shifted herself around. Like she was uncomfortable. "Morning, Evie," she said, not even bothering to whisper. She stared off in a corner and smoked an unfiltered, roll-your-own cigarette. Something she never does unless she's not at home. Can't at her place. Mustn't. Against the law.

"Aunt Odie," I said, stretching my toes toward her, lifting my fingertips to the ceiling. "You're spreading secondhand smoke to me, the birthday girl."

"I know that." She grinned, stubbed the butt out in an

ashtray that rested on her belly, shifted again. "Get on outta bed. We got big things to do today. Miles to go before we eat."

The curtains behind her moved in a breeze that couldn't be there, seeing the windows were shut.

I blinked at the almost sun that peered into my room.

Let out a sigh.

Stretched again.

In just three days, I would start tenth grade, and I didn't think I could stand it. Not the excitement. Not the scary parts.

Aunt Odie kept not looking at me, like she was mustering courage. Something tapped at the back of my skull.

"Ugh," I said. "You know I got school coming up."

My aunt gave me a somber look. Bits of the sun touched at her hair, making the gray look silver.

August 25 always arrives too quick—my birthday or not. The start of school.

Again.

Every year.

No matter what.

Except Saturdays and Sundays.

Of course.

"Yes sirree, buddy," Aunt Odie said. "You heading on back means I'll be losing my best worker."

I couldn't speak. I wanted to say, *I'm ready*. But all that came out was the "I'm." What I wanted to say was, *I'm ready to go with you on my birthday adventure but not to high school.*

4

What I wanted to say was, *Why do I have to grow up so fast?*

I flopped back, turned over, and buried my face into the cool side of the pillow.

Sure, I wanted to go on off to another year of high school. What teenager doesn't, right?

We're supposed to *want* to start a new adventure.

I swallowed back a big old gob of spit. I *didn't* want to go too.

I felt uneasy all the way to the core.

To the center.

Blech. An institution of higher learning. Good if I wanted to head to college. Except this also meant—

No more freedom.

No more sweet Baby Lucy.

No more sleep as long as I wanted.

I rolled onto my back. Stared at the ceiling.

And no more running off with Aunt Odie before the sun got itself all the way up. It was sad.

Sad.

Aunt Odie let out a rumble of a laugh. "Quit your whining," she said, though I hadn't uttered a word.

I squinched my eyebrows at her.

"We got us plans," she said. "Your momma said we could head out on our little trip as long as I got you back to the house by the time Baby Lucy wakes up. So hurry on up, girly. The Cadillac's all cooled off on the inside. Breakfast sandwiches waiting in tinfoil. Big jug of sweet tea. It's time for us to git."

I rubbed at my eyes.

"Happy birthday, Evie," Aunt Odie said, just like a best friend would. Her voice all honey.

"Why, thank you," I said, and thought to bow, but bowing is not that easy when you're lying in bed.

With a grunt, my aunt pushed herself out of the chair and set it to rocking. The curtains waved and rippled. She caught the ashtray before it slipped to the floor. Pinched the cigarette out all the way. "Number fifteen. The most important celebration ever in a Messenger's life. Not including marriage, births, and deaths."

"Yes, ma'am," I said, and waited for her to leave so I could get dressed.

2

I almost didn't have the chance to go to the potty, that's how quick Aunt Odie ran me out of my sleeping house, all quiet.

I'm surprised she let me change out of my jammies.

Shorts.

T-shirt.

Pulled my way-too-curly hair back in a ponytail in my bathroom. I could hear Aunt Odie way off in another part of our home.

"Closed-toe shoes, girly. No flip-flops today."

"Yes, ma'am," I said. I hip-hopped down the hall, slipping on my tennies. Past the family portraits of the Messengers way on back to black-and-white and grainy sepia.

"I tell you," Aunt Odie said as we went outside. The weather held a full house as far as humidity was concerned. I tried to shrug away from the suffocating feeling. Impossible. "We got us a morning storm on its way."

I glanced at the sky. Clouds, dark and threatening, swirled everywhere. The air dripped moisture. The grass was so damp the dew made my shoes wet, then my toes, straight through the canvas.

"Shoulda let me wear flip-flops," I said.

Across the street I eyed Buddy McKay's house. He is the cutest thing in all a New Smyrna Beach.

And nasty, too. In a really cute sorta way.

Tried to kiss me the day I moved in this here place just over a year ago.

I sighed, remembering. Then sighed again.

I'd almost let him. His hand warm on my arm. His breath all peppermint.

"Closed toes for today." Aunt Odie unlocked the car from where she balanced on one foot on the front porch. Like she was a huge flamingo. One wearing a perm. The petunias smelled the yard up. The magnolias, both fat with blossoms, kept their flowers and fragrance all closed up.

"Get on in there," she said. "You know my corns slow me."

I did. "Ooooeee," I said, fastening the seat belt and making sure it was snug but not snug enough to choke the life out of me. "Something smells good." My stomach rumbled, agreeing.

A picnic basket sat at my feet.

Fifteen.

I leaned my head back on the soft leather of the Cadillac.

Closed my eyes.

Breathed deep the smell of breakfast.

"See your own future," I said. I used the most command-
ing voice I have. "What lies ahead for you, Evie Montgomery
Messenger?"

I needed to make my family proud or just be done with it,
which I knew might prove easier.

But there was no future. All I saw was the back of my
eyelids.

3

Aunt Odie is the best cook there is in all Florida. Maybe Georgia and Alabama and Louisiana, too.

She makes everything from scratch, even her own mixes for things like cakes and biscuits and brownies. She sells the mixes down to the Publix supermarkets. And lots of other places. Like the Piggly Wiggly. And Walmart. Plus to grocery stores in the other states I have mentioned.

The whole summer long, every Monday, Wednesday, Friday, and some Saturdays I help my great-aunt measure and stir and package—right there in her huge professional kitchen, the biggest part of her house.

She pays me seven dollars a case of product, which is a pretty good hourly rate. No taxes pulled out. Straight under the table.

I'm saving up for a Harley-Davidson motorcycle.

But there are production rules. Hair in a net. Wear food-grade gloves. No rock-and-roll hoochie-koo music.

The most important thing about mixing mixes, though,

is love. Love in every box. That means I have to think good thoughts while I work.

Can't mix when I'm agitated or angry or feeling down in the dumps.

Can't mix if I didn't sleep good, or even had nightmares.

Most of the time it's not hard to do. I'm a happy girl.

"People know," Aunt Odie says, her hands laced over her belly. "They know if we think good or bad things. And Mixed with Love Is the Secret Ingredient."

I believe her. She has the business that brings in oodles of money that affords her to live in this fancy-schmancy neighborhood. I'm only a helper. Plus, it says those words on every box.

Right now I was eating an Aunt Carolina (yep, Aunt Odie doesn't use her own name, *and* she didn't make me wait miles to eat. In fact, we were still in the driveway.) Drop Biscuit split in half, slathered with honey, and topped with grilled ham and an over-medium egg. Just like what is pictured on the packaging.

The sandwich was still hot. Smelled like heaven with a dash of pepper.

Aunt Odie provided a bib and plenty of napkins and a quart jar of fresh cold tea, lemon slices bobbing in there plus a cyclone of sugar to make it taste perfect.

And there were hash browns.

"Your momma knows I'm feeding you and all, but *she* intends to make a day of it after our adventure."

Aunt Odie eased into the car.

All the windows were fogged up. Even the ones in the back. She flipped on the defroster.

Fastened her seat belt.

Turned to me and smiled.

"I put on my JC Penney girdle for you, Evie."

I dabbed at my lips with the fancy birthday napkin.

"That ol' rubber thing I pulled out of your bottom drawer the other day?"

"Yup."

I swallowed my bite of food. No wonder she was squiggling around. "I thought you said you hadn't seen that since the seventies."

"That's right. I look any thinner?"

"Sure," I said, after a glance. She didn't.

So you know, I'm not supposed to lie when I'm working on the mixes either.

Aunt Odie wrestled with the steering wheel, moving it this way and that, settling with her stomach snug against the wheel.

"Et's-lay o-gay," Aunt Odie said. Aunt Odie speaks perfect pig Latin. All my great-aunts do. I'm only partially proficient. "Edal-pay oo-tay ee-thay etal-may."

Then she tore out of the driveway, driving as fast backing up as she does when she puts the car into *go*.

"It might be there is nothing," she said when we sat in the middle of the road, staring at my house. For someone itching to go, she wasn't driving. "Now lookit. You know there is the Messenger oddball who has no skill. Happens every onct in a while."

I thought I might choke. "Well, thanks."

"I'm just sayin'."

"I know."

She was talking about the Gift.

In my heart I was torn. It wasn't what I wanted. Healing like Momma. Cooking like Aunt Odie. Hair like Aunt Carol.

And I didn't want to be an oddball, either.

Could I do that? Not be like anyone else in the family? Hmmm. It was scary, but I kinda liked the idea. Being . . . being me.

"But if there is something in there"—Aunt Odie tapped at her head, then at her heart—"my friend down to Cassadaga can pull the Gift right outta you."

"Lookit," I said. Worry fell over me like a shawl.

"Lookit nothing," Aunt Odie said. "I know you're nervous. But . . ." She stopped talking long enough to take a gigantic bite from her own breakfast sandwich. Egg dripped on the bib she rested on her bosoms.

"There's no denying it, Evie. We gotta do what we gotta do. Messengers are here . . ."

". . . to bless others with their skills," we said together.

"Right," Aunt Odie said. She sighed. Maybe because I had the right answer. Maybe because that sandwich tasted so good.

A raindrop the size of a nickel smacked onto the windshield. One pinged on the roof.

I said, "You know you don't like driving in weather." No need to argue about the other stuff. She wasn't listening.

Aunt Odie put the car in gear. "You're right. So we better get going."

Buddy McKay came outside to deliver newspapers, his hair like a rat's nest, which seems impossible seeing it's a pretty close cut. He's sixteen. Too old for me, my momma would say.

His lips looked ripe enough to kiss.

He licked those ripe lips in a downright sexy way at me as Aunt Odie roared down the street, lifting her sandwich in a salute. I stared out the window at Buddy, craning my neck to watch him till he was nothing but the shadow of a figure.

Before we even got to the four-way stop, the sky opened up wide like a yawn and poured what seemed like the whole Atlantic Ocean on us. Aunt Odie ate on. And drove, too.

4

We almost couldn't see Cassadaga. That's how black the storm was. The streetlights were on, looking like blurry pumpkins the closer we got to them.

"This place ain't but a mile long," Aunt Odie said. She muttered the words at the steamed-up windshield, wiping at the glass with the back of her hand. She wore a bit of egg on her chin. Now we drove eight miles an hour and that was still too fast.

I clutched at my seat belt. Tried to stare through the rain. Breakfast swam in my gut.

"It's on the right."

"I can't see a thing," I said.

"Look harder."

"I'm looking."

The heavens split, turning angry clouds bright with lightning, showing the sky to be deep purple, not black or gray at all.

"There," she said, and would have pointed, I thought, if she hadn't been so afraid to turn the wheel free.

Pale light bloomed in the rain. Blue as an eye.

A chill ran over my body, like I had taken off my skin, thrown it in the deep freeze, then slipped the flesh back on.

"What?" I said. "I mean, who?"

Aunt Odie didn't say anything. Just drove through the flood, that had to be high as the hubcaps.

She pulled into the underwater driveway, smiling like she found sunken treasure. Which was almost the case, seeing the water standing in the yard. Good thing this—what? place of business? house?—was up off the ground on cinder blocks. Kept the interior dry. Anything tucked beneath the place, though, was washed away, sure. Hope they didn't lay out fishing poles and gear there. Hope there was a shed for the hoe and shovel. But maybe people who saw the future knew that already and had moved anything of value to the front porch.

"What a day to turn fifteen," Aunt Odie said, giving me the ol' eyeball. Like maybe it was *my* fault the rain came and not a habit of Florida weather.

"If I had a choice," I said, fingering the door handle, "I woulda chose May. Like Lucy. Or September, like Momma. That would make me a Libra. Not a stinky ol' Virgo."

The Virgin, I thought, then remembered Buddy's hand on my arm, all warm. My breath caught.

"Oh, you choose," Aunt Odie said, then hefted herself outta the car. I heard her splashing around. Probably wishing for rain boots. "Birth and death ain't left to chance."

"Sure they are," I said without conviction, then opened the door and looked at the swirling water at my feet. I expected to see a flounder or a catfish. There weren't any. "I need a life preserver."

"Time's a-wasting," Aunt Odie said, "and this girdle is squeezing the life outta me. Plus, Sandy's waiting to watch *One Life to Live*."

Sandy is Aunt Odie's best friend from high school. Once every two weeks they watch all their favorite soaps together. Sandy was coming in this evening after my party.

"This is my birthday celebration," I said. Thunder crashed, moving the air around us. I felt all grumpy between the eyes. Raindrops splashed around me. Patted my head. Wet my shoulders. Wouldn't be making any mixes in this all-the-sudden mood. I squinted. Now that I was out of the car, my feet soaked (not just the toes), I could see the blue light was a sign that read OPEN. Water came right up to my ankles.

"That's right," Aunt Odie said. "It's this storm *and* this girdle that's getting to me. I'm sorry, sugar." She sloshed through the yard, splashing me as she came nearer. Rain popped all around us.

No girdle to explain my poutiness. Couldn't blame the storm. What had descended upon me?

"Love you," she said. "You know you are my most favorite niece."

I grinned, my mood almost switching to happiness

17

despite the foul weather. "And about the only one you have."

Aunt Odie offered me a hug and I took it. Then we walked through the surge that felt cold as the tea we'd been drinking, and up the steps where Aunt Odie plucked two unopened hibiscus flowers from the bushes that fronted the porch. She tucked one behind her ear and motioned for me to do the same. The flower dripped the surge down the side of her face. I'm not sure she even noticed.

5

Who would paint their business this purple color?

I went to knock on the door.

"Coming," someone said.

"Wait"—I pulled on Aunt Odie's caftan—"is that . . . is that a man's voice?"

"Yes, it is," he said. The door opened wide, and a man as big and tall as the doorway stood before us. "Unusual, right? A male medium who happens to be the size of a giant."

"Umm," I said.

Aunt Odie offered her hand to him. "Paulie," she said. "He is a jack-of-all-trades. Has a Gift that shames most."

"Odie, don't!" Paulie said, but I could see he loved her bragging on him.

"I was thinking . . ." My voice was drowned out by the rain on the tin roof.

"What everyone thinks," Paulie said. "I should be a woman with kohl eyes wearing a frock like this." He eyed Aunt Odie up and down. She beamed. Petted her dress.

Past Paulie, the room was like a hole. Maybe even darker because of the morning outside. The blue of the OPEN sign made the furniture look like monsters—or monsters like the furniture. A high-backed sofa. Three chairs. Was that a bear in the corner or a hutch? Would this medium turn on a light or what?

"Have a seat," Paulie said when we crowded into the foyer. He gestured to two chairs, then moved himself faster than I thought someone his size could, to his own chair, where he plopped with a sigh behind a small table. I could hardly see him, it was so dark. I could hardly see Aunt Odie, who was close enough to touch.

We sat. Pulled in tighter.

Outside it sounded like the storm stood right over us. When lightning split the sky, it was as if someone had flashed an old-fashioned camera in the room. Then slammed a fist onto the roof.

The smell of rain almost covered the smell of cinnamon.

"Those are for later," Paulie said.

"Excuse me?" I said.

"Let me hold your hand."

Aunt Odie giggled.

She extended her fingers to him.

Did she . . . did Aunt Odie have a crush on Paulie? I looked from my aunt to Paulie to Aunt Odie again. Did they? Like each other?

"Not you, Odie. Evie," Paulie said. "I need to see *her* hand if you want any help here. I've already looked at yours." In the darkness they stared at each other. Smiling.

"Of course," Aunt Odie said. She sounded like a movie actress.

Just like that I thought about Buddy. His hair black as this room. Eyes too brown to look at. Would he ever smile at me the way these two smiled at each other? Did I want him to? Was I too young for a serious sixteen-year-old boyfriend?

"So there's someone you're interested in?" Paulie's touch was like electricity.

"Not really," I said. My face burned, and not because I'd lied. I hadn't. I wasn't sure how I felt about Buddy.

Except I wanted him to kiss me.

But I didn't let him.

Maybe I never would.

Who knew?

"Pay attention," Paulie said. "You're thinking of everything but what we're supposed to be doing here."

I tried to focus.

Aunt Odie shifted in her seat. Thunder shook the walls around us. The line of pictures hanging there chattered. "It's her birthday, Paulie," Aunt Odie said. "Her *special* birthday."

"I know that, Odie," Paulie said, like the news wasn't fabulous or news at all. "Let's see." He bowed his head. Fingered the silk of the tablecloth.

How could he see anything, my palm included, in this gloom?

"Sometimes I know things," I said, trying to be helpful when Paulie didn't speak at once. "Or I dream stuff."

"You don't need to tell me anything." In the near darkness he peered into my eyes. His skin seemed to glow.

I blinked.

"Besides, everyone can do that," he said, "if they pay attention. Nothing unique about knowing or dreaming."

Lightning hit the house then. For a moment I was stone deaf.

Aunt Odie let out a scream, but I almost couldn't hear her. For sure I saw her mouth go wide.

My fingers tingled like the electricity had traveled through my body.

The room lit up bright as day. I saw us all in there, like a photograph. Like I stared at a picture of the room instead of participated.

Paulie and I gripped hands, and he stared in that bright light, right into my eyes. Into my brain and heart and maybe into my blood vessels.

His mouth dropped open. His fingers squeezed mine.

"Ouch," I said.

All that in less than the blink of an eye.

Paulie stood then, without warning. Knocked his chair to the floor behind him. Stumbled. "Wow. Whoa. No. Nonono."

"What?" Aunt Odie said.

"Nothing," he said. He turned from us, took a couple of steps toward a darkened doorway. "I see nothing special about her as far as a Gift." His voice was two octaves higher, at least.

Aunt Odie didn't speak.

Neither did I. Had some ancestor heard me wonder about not wanting the family Gift?

Then Aunt Odie said, "Well."

My heart fluttered.

"So."

I was . . . what? Embarrassed? "I didn't really think . . . ," I said, whispering.

"I see."

I was an oddball. A Messenger oddball. In the darkness I accepted the fact. There's an oddball in every family. Sometimes two. Aunt Odie said so.

Now she stood. "Are you sure, Paulie? She seems different from the others." She worried at the hibiscus she'd stuck behind her ear. Mine, I noticed, was in full bloom, openthroated, on the table.

"You have to go." Paulie waved a hand around. "I mean, I have to go. There are cinnamon rolls on the kitchen counter. I made them for you. From one of your mixes. You know the way, Odie."

He reached behind him and seemed to pull a raincoat from thin air. Then he was gone.

I swallowed.

I hadn't wanted the Gift.

Not really.

Ask anyone. The Gift's trouble with a capital *T*. Or maybe I should say a capital *G*.

Still, a bit of disappointment settled in my stomach, right near the over-medium egg. It squiggled around in the yolk, then rested in the hash browns.

You think all your life you're going to be something. Have a talent. Be able to, I don't know, get rid of warts by buying them for a few pennies (Great-Grandmother Price) or make people fat using a turnip and a little candle wax (Mary, my cousin twice removed).

You think you're going to be a Messenger woman when you turn fifteen, and even if you sorta want to be like your friends at school, you accept there's a part of yourself that's different.

But no.

I wished it and I got it.

I was an oddball.

6

Me and Aunt Odie stood on the porch a long minute.

The blue OPEN light went out.

Overhead, the storm eased up. The sun tried to push through but couldn't make a break past the clouds. I smelled wood rot.

I stepped into the yard as Aunt Odie said, "I don't think so," and plowed on back into Paulie's house. Not even knocking, mind you.

"He's gone," I said. "He took that raincoat—"

"Like hell he is."

The door slammed behind Aunt Odie.

A breeze rushed past. Tugged at my curls. Swirled. Twisted. Tried to pull me with it.

Then, "Now, Odie," I heard Paulie say. His voice was a whine.

"You saw something," she said. "I saw you see it. The lightning. That blast. I *saw* you see!"

I was a tree rooted to the porch. Listening in. Mist swirled around. Crawled up my legs. Fog rose from the earth. Tangled with the breeze.

"You know I didn't."

"I know you did."

There was a shuffling sound and I heard whispering, but I couldn't make out what was being said. I leaned closer to the open window. The curtains from inside strained against the screen to get to where I stood.

"What?" Aunt Odie said. The sound of her voice stilled my blood. "What? Are you kidding?"

The door slammed open, bouncing off the wall, and my aunt hightailed it outta that place, like someone had set her afire.

Just in case Beelzebub had been revealed to her, I followed Aunt Odie lickety-split.

7

Water stood high in the streets.

Aunt Odie drove faster than a bat outta hell. Whatever Paulie had told her had scared her good.

Scared me, too, though I had no idea what I was afraid of. A fist beat at the inside of my throat.

Seeing the whole town of soothsayers, palm readers, and fortune-tellers is only a mile long, we were out of Cassadaga in less than forty seconds. Water sprayed from each side of the car like waves.

"Hope you don't get us trapped here," I said. "Hope you don't stall out the motor." The trees reached for the car. "This is one scary place. Especially when it's storming." I wanted to ask my own *what*? Say my own *Tell me*. But I didn't. Instead I just warned her.

But Aunt Odie didn't slow down.

"You could stall out the motor. You could hydroplane."

There was a dead armadillo looking a lot like a half-inflated soccer ball floating on our side of the road.

"We could end up like him."

Not a word.

Palm fronds edged closer to the asphalt.

At long last I sat back in my seat after mentioning every possible car problem—none of which Aunt Odie took to heart, and that made it seem maybe I didn't have the gift of seeing car misfortunes—and held on for dear life.

"Not so sure"—Aunt Odie mumbled under her breath and gripped the steering wheel with one hand—"I have given you the best birthday present after all."

Those words scared me even more.

She's been waiting to give me this gift for 364 days. Since the day after I turned fourteen. (She got me three biddies last year. They lay eggs now that they're grown, pale-pink eggs, every day for the last six months. They follow me around the yard when I go out back of my aunt's house, where they have a miniature home that looks like Aunt Odie's, including a long, screened-in porch area. We stir up the Aunt Carolina mixes with those eggs. And plain fry them too. I love all three of my chickens, though I must admit Nina is my favorite, with Santa Maria and Pinta both coming in a close second. Of course, I would never tell any of them how I feel.)

"Now what? Now what?"

"Now what *what*?" I said.

Then I knew. I saw it on her face.

"It was the storm," I said. My words came out a whisper filled with gravel. "Wasn't it? The storm had something to do with my birthday."

Aunt Odie took in a breath.

"I never did tell you about my old auntie Doris, did I?"

I swallowed. Shook my head.

"Didn't think so." Aunt Odie took in another deep breath. "Sure wish I knew how to do the sign of the cross, but we Jehovah's Witnesses don't do that."

Jehovah's Witnesses also don't celebrate birthdays, either, but I said nothing.

"Well?" I said after a couple of miles.

Aunt Odie looked over at me with one eye. "Well what?"

"You gonna tell me about her?"

"Who?"

"Auntie Doris?" Ahead of us the sky was as bright as a jewel. All the clouds, dark as a witch, traveled toward the gulf.

Aunt Odie sort of crossed herself in an odd diamond shape, adding in a few extra swipes at her chest. "To be safe," she said.

Then she looked at me with both eyeballs.

"Not till tonight."

"Of course."

Aunt Odie pulled over on the side of the road, right close to a ditch where water ran fast toward the ocean.

"I am gonna tell you something, though."

She shut the engine off.

"All right."

"It is high time I told you," Aunt Odie said, "what my Gift is."

8

Aunt Odie leaned close. She whispered at me. Her breath smelled like honey. It always smells like honey.

"I get my recipes from dreams."

"I know that."

She sat back in the car seat. Her hand rested on the steering wheel.

"From the dead."

"I know that, too."

"Written out on three-by-five recipe cards."

I blinked, nodded all slow. That I did *not* know.

"Longhand. In my head. That's my Gift. The recipes aren't my own, but given to me." She closed her eyes. Patted at her forehead, then spread her hands out like maybe I should take something from her.

"This is how the Gift works for us. It helps us. Or helps us help others."

"Okay," I said.

"I make a pretty penny selling these mixes, which benefits the entire family."

This is true.

Aunt Odie helped me and Momma for a good long time. Let us stay with her all my life while Momma took care of me and worked off hours at the 5 & Dime.

Then she met JimDaddy, who is a wealthy contractor. And here we all are.

"My mixes," Aunt Odie said with reverence, "help otherwise cooking-challenged women please their families with tasty dishes that taste homemade."

Like the commercials on TV say, I thought, but I said, "Yes, they do."

"What?"

"Taste homemade. And help."

My aunt nodded. "I know. It's part of the Gift."

"Should we git on home?"

"Sometimes," Aunt Odie said, "these Gifts are not what we expect. Or hope. Sometimes we have to make them what they become."

I faced front in the car. Stared out the steamy window. "Why're you telling me this? We both saw what happened with your friend Paulie. There's nothing here."

Aunt Odie didn't say another word. Just started the car and drove us on home.

9

Momma, JimDaddy, and Baby Lucy were right there, on the porch, waiting for us.

All smiles.

"Well?" Momma said, eyebrows raised.

"Didn't go so great," I said.

"Later," Aunt Odie said.

"Now hold on," Momma said. "What do you mean?"

"I mean," I said, "Paulie didn't see nothing."

JimDaddy watched us with an almost interest. Baby Lucy teethed on a wrapped present.

"And I said later," Aunt Odie said.

"Nothing?" Momma said.

"Nothing," I said.

"This is talk for when we are alone." Aunt Odie said the words all serious and Momma didn't question again. Instead, she hesitated then grabbed me in a hug. Smiled bright enough to light up a room. "Now don't you worry."

"I'm not." Oddball. Though I was. Aunt Odie seemed near to having a conniption.

Momma kissed the side of my head. "Now lookit. Not everyone gets this."

"The Messenger women do," I said. "That's why we don't change our names at marriage."

What could Momma say to that?

Or JimDaddy, who didn't argue even a second when Momma told him our family rules.

What would Buddy say about that? I let out a nervous giggle at that random thought.

"This. Is. A. Conversation. For. Later. On."

But Momma, who loves Aunt Odie more than I do, said, "We knew she wasn't getting any signs something was coming." Momma whispered like I wasn't standing right there. "Not like the rest of us."

Aunt Odie flopped in an Adirondack and set to fanning herself with the skirt of her dress. "What does it matter what I say?"

"So," JimDaddy said. "Let's get on with this." He thrust Baby Lucy, her hair hanging in tiny curls though she isn't even nine months old, into my arms. "She's been waiting on you, Evie."

"See what she got you," Momma said, her arm still around my shoulder.

I grinned. "Okay."

Aunt Odie was three shades paler. Sweating, too. (Even though she is a big girl, my aunt never sweats. Not even on a baking day when you could roast meat outside. Or in.)

"You okay?" I asked.

She nodded.

"Then my present," JimDaddy said.

Gift. Shmift. Ffift.

He placed a kiss on my forehead. His hands shook and his lips were dry. Momma patted at my arm.

Had they slept right through that storm?

Water stood in the front yard. The petunias looked soggy.

Across the street at Buddy's place, there wasn't anyone even moving. Not that I could see, I mean.

Momma, her face changing from worried to excited, said, "Mine last of all."

Baby Lucy held a cell phone and JimDaddy had two cases for me plus a gift card to Wet Seal.

Momma jumped a little, bursting to give me her news. "A party." She danced me around in a tight circle on the porch. JimDaddy stared off across the yard. His hair caught the sun, making it look more blond than normal. Baby Lucy bounced around in my arms. I pulled a bit of damp cardboard from her mouth. She grinned at me. Would she be an oddball too? Or keep red ants and other pests far from our yards and homes?

I said, "A party?" What I wanted to say was, *Who will I invite?* when Momma said, "I done sent everything out. Plus got back the RSVPs. You have five people visiting this evening, so I thought we could get you over to Aunt Carol's place and let her give you a makeover."

Momma folded her hands under her chin like she had finished praying.

"But Momma," I said, 'cause she and I hadn't been here long enough for me to have one friend, much less five. Me and Momma moved in with JimDaddy right before Baby Lucy was born. This change of venue shoved me to a brand-new high school. Left my old friends behind. Another scary reason to back off higher education. Who could be coming? My stomach frumphed at the thought.

"You love it?" Momma asked. "You love your presents?"

Momma and Aunt Odie looked at me, the baby too. Talk about three peas in a pod. I said, "Yes, ma'am, you know I do."

Then we *all* jumped all over the porch, this way and that, while Aunt Odie panted and fanned, hair moving like it breathed.

10

In my room, I paced.

Back and forth.

I didn't want a party.

For me, the family—*my* family—was good enough party people.

But try to tell a Messenger anything. They hear only what they want to hear. So Momma swooped me up for a late afternoon lunch, and a little bit of school clothes shopping, and then carried me off to Aunt Carol, who patted at my hair with both hands. While I sat in front of the mirror and avoided my own gaze. Sheesh.

"It's growing long, Evie. You want I should cut it?"

She motioned with her fingers—shoulder length. Behind me, her own hair stood out like a tornado had ripped through her shop. Momma's did the same.

"I don't think so," Momma said.

"Me neither," I said.

"Good," Aunt Carol said. She applied a little goop, pulled

out the curling iron, steamed and twirled, then gave my hair a pat, pat, pat. Right above both ears.

She turned the chair, making me face her.

Aunt Carol, three years younger than Aunt Odie, put her hands to my cheeks. "A little makeup and not one boy who visits tonight will be able to look away."

"Boys?" I asked.

Momma yelped. "Surprise!" She did a bit of a jig.

"I *am* surprised," I said. *And a little humiliated, too*, I wanted to say. But who can pop her momma's happiness bubble with that kind of grouchy attitude? Yup. No mixing mixes today. And maybe no mixing at mixers. I sighed.

Aunt Carol got out a tray with so many colors it put a good evening rainbow to shame.

"A little bit of purple," she said, closing my eyelid with her pinkie finger. "Makes green eyes look greener. Some gold." She stared me right in the one eyeball. "So everyone knows who the birthday girl is."

I swallowed. I could smell perm solution. Bobby Rae rang up a customer, then slapped his hands clean after putting the money in the register.

"How was your trip with Odie?" Momma asked. She read a *People* magazine. A super-old Brad Pitt stepped out of the ocean on the cover.

I shrugged.

"Don't move," Aunt Carol said. "You wanna look like a

ho?" Her hands were cool and not shaking even one tiny bit, the way mine do when I apply mascara.

"No, ma'am," I said. 'Cause I didn't. "Aunt Odie was sure Paulie would be able to tell me if I got any of the family Gifts. But he didn't say anything. Just rushed us outta his house like that." I snapped my fingers. The plastic apron, the color of a good black eye, waved with my movements.

Aunt Carol stopped applying makeup. Momma waited.

I stared at them in the mirror. Across the salon from us was Judy, giving someone a perm. And Maggie Moo helped a little old lady over to a sink so they could get her hair done.

Momma said, "She took you awful early to see Paulie."

Momma knew Paulie?

"Tell me about it."

"She's always the most anxious," Momma said, and Aunt Carol agreed with a nod. "Always has been."

"So what happened?" This was Aunt Carol.

I wanted to shrug, and perhaps it was the best time to, because Aunt Carol was looking at Momma now.

They were communicating the way the Messengers do. Like someone (me) wouldn't see them and wouldn't get whatever they were talking about was awful important, otherwise words would be coming outta their mouths.

"And?" Momma said.

"And nothing," I said. "Like I told you, Momma." I gave

them both a trembly smile. What was wrong with me? I was okay not having a Messenger Gift. Who cared? "Looks like I lucked out. Ain't nothing but a thing."

"Hurry it up, Aunt Carol," Momma said. Her face changed from concerned to super concerned. Like she had realized something big. And then, "Can I borrow your cell phone, Evie?"

Just like that my hands started shaking. "Quit trying to scare me," I said, and retrieved the phone from my pocket. I handed it over to Momma. Don't ask me why she doesn't have a phone of her own. It's her goal to be the only person in the world to not have one. Up till this morning, there were two of us.

"You know all this," I said. "You and Aunt Odie went on forever about it this morning."

Momma didn't answer.

Aunt Carol went back to working on my face. She was silent now. Listening in on Momma, no doubt. I was too.

The salon felt all the sudden hot and sticky. I wanted to throw the apron aside and go stand in front of the air conditioner. Would that mess up my straightened hair? Why was that little lady talking so much to Maggie Moo? And what was Momma finding out, anyway?

After a long minute Momma said, kinda loud, "We all got Gifts, Evie. Every one of us. Some more powerful than others." Then she glanced at me and Aunt Carol in the mirror and left the shop so she could make her call in private.

11

Momma has the huge Messenger eyes and the hair that looks like someone's been teasing it too hard. Her legs are thin and long and so are her arms, and when people see us together, the really old ones ask if we are twins.

"Separated at birth," Momma always says.

On the way home from the beauty parlor, she refused to talk to me about anything but the party. And even then she was scant on the details.

"Just you wait," she said.

12

From the road I could see there was something amiss at the Messenger-Fletcher household. There were people at my home. One girl even walked into the backyard through the side gate.

My stomach tried to squeeze out my mouth but I swallowed it, gagging only once.

"Momma," I said. Panic came out with the word.

My mother switched off the car and turned to face me. "Baby girl," she said. "You know you are the love of my life. This is good for you." She stared off over my shoulder so hard I worried maybe she'd caught a glimpse of my Gift. Something Paulie couldn't see. I checked out the window behind me.

Nothing but a dusky sky and dragonflies zipping over the yard.

I swallowed again.

"I don't think this is such a good idea. You know how scared I get. You know how shy I am."

Momma nodded. "I do, Evie. But this is your special day.

You are fifteen." She said it like I would be president. "And that means something in our family. The party is waiting on you. It's almost eight."

I closed my eyes, remembering Aunt Odie hightailing it away from Paulie's place. Then remembered all that private phone talking Momma had done in Aunt Carol's salon. And her refusing to tell me anything at all.

"You gotta step forward and get counted."

My voice came out a whisper. "I don't want to."

Momma pressed a kiss to my forehead. "You look gorgy, baby girl," she said. "Let's get going."

So we got, whether I wanted to or not.

Sigh.

These Messengers.

13

JimDaddy and Baby Lucy stood right inside the living room under the chandelier that sent sparkles of light like fairies onto all the walls. The guests included—how could it be—my very own best friend Pearl from where we used to live what seemed an eternity ago!

Pearl squealed and ran at me. We hugged so tight I thought my eyeballs might pop outta my head.

"What are you doing home?" I said, breathless. My face was going to break in half I smiled so much.

"I'm here for this, of course," Pearl said, spreading her arms wide. My best friend is named Pearl on accounta she was born with a mouthful of teeth that looked just like pearls. Her momma said to my momma (who was in the delivery room because her momma and my momma are best friends too), "Gotta make the best of it," about all those teeth. My momma had agreed and told me later Pearl scared the bejesus out of her every time the baby smiled until she was two years old and was *supposed* to have some of those chompers.

44

"Love your makeup," Pearl said now. Her teeth gleamed. They look great, seeing she's grown into them. "Aunt Carol did the same look for me one hour before you got in there." Pearl's been calling my aunts her aunts all our lives. She closed her eyes and I saw silver sparkle through the purple and pink.

"Beautiful," I said, and hugged her tight again, whispering, "I am so glad you are back from Wilderness Camp."

JimDaddy said, "Evie, you know Buddy. This here is Vera, Charles, and that there is Julius."

"Hey, y'all," I said, and they all mumbled back a hey except Buddy, who said, "I get the first kiss."

He was so good-looking and his eyes were so brown I almost said, *When do we start?* but Momma stared at me with a fake smile on her face and JimDaddy pulled Buddy to the corner where my stepfather had set up his electric guitar and microphone. The two of them talked until it was time to sing "Happy Birthday." Buddy nodded like a bobblehead.

No Gift and no birthday kiss tonight. How could it be? Life was only half fair.

14

While JimDaddy tuned his guitar and while Momma had everyone pile fresh ingredients on their individual pizza crusts (another Aunt Odie secret recipe), I excused myself to my bedroom to take a deep breath and try and calm the nerves.

I eased the door shut behind me and leaned against it.

A girl stood in the corner of my room. The one I'd seen going through the gate to the backyard.

"Erp," I said, startled.

She flapped her hand at me. "Sorry, Evie," she said. "I shoulda been there when your JimDaddy was making introductions, but I can't hang out with Justin."

"Oh."

"It makes me sad."

"Um."

She pulled her blacker-than-black hair back into a ponytail. It glittered in the lights from the special-order pink chandelier. "I'm Tommie."

"Okay."

"Sorry for not meeting you in the living room. It looks good, doesn't it?"

"What?" I asked, and then said, "That's okay."

What was she doing in here? And without my permission. And what was she talking about?

"Evie!" Momma called. "Come on and make your pizza!"

I went to the heart-shaped mirror that hung over the dresser. My hair was still okay, styled in a way I would never be able to do myself. But my eyes looked too big. Surprised. And why not? There was a stranger in my bedroom.

"Evie?" Momma again.

I looked over my shoulder. "We better go," I said, "or my momma is gonna have an infarction."

Tommie laughed, a soft sound that was almost sad. "In a minute," she said. "I promise."

"But, ummm, everyone's out here. That's where the party is."

Tommie's eyes filled with tears, making the blue color intensify. Her skin was so pale I knew she'd sunburn the moment she got out in full day unless she had on SPF 8000.

"I'm not sure why I'm so emotional. We used to go out," she said. She sat at the edge of my bed and wept into her hands. She looked too young to date to me, but maybe her momma didn't care so much. What was a kid like her doing at my party? "And now everyone in the neighborhood is ignoring me. When I came tonight, I thought I could handle it. But I can't." She cried some more, her hair falling forward like a shroud.

Well, this was awkward.

"Evie," Momma called. "Your guests are waiting for you."

"Okay," I said to Tommie. "You can stay in here for a little bit. I guess."

She looked up at me, her face filled with thankfulness, then stood, went to the window, and turned back to me. "Are you sure? I'd really appreciate it."

I wasn't sure, but what could I do?

"Yeah," I said, and left Tommie in the corner of my room, staring out the window into the growing darkness.

15

I scrunched into the kitchen with everyone. Julius tipped his head in my direction. "Nice to meet you, Evie," he said.

So this was Tommie's old boyfriend. Cute, yes. Why had he dumped her? I'd try to find out tonight.

Buddy slipped up between me and the boy Tommie was worried about. He smelled like soap. Buddy, not Julius.

"Hey, birthday girl," Buddy said. I glanced at him, quick-like. He almost smiled.

"Hey." I felt my face turn red as cake batter after Aunt Odie has been liberal with the food coloring. The thought of almost letting him kiss me made my stomach fall in on itself like a failed soufflé. I knew for sure my makeup did not go with embarrassment. I needed to get ahold of myself.

"I got something for you later." Buddy kept trying to look me in the eye, but I was too embarrassed. Plus, he whispered awful loud.

Charles let out a "jeez," then wandered over when Momma

said, "Cheese is right here. And sardines are real good on a pizza, you know."

Pearl grabbed me by the elbow. Grinned right in my face, then gave me a little wave. "Don't you dare take my best friend away from me! We have been apart all summer."

"I got a new phone," I said. Where had I put that thing? "Now we can text each other."

Pearl whooped. Her mother is more accepting of modern times than mine. And no, Momma wouldn't let me get my own cellular device before, even if I paid. Didn't matter if I had the funds. "No need," Momma had said, "of spending the few hours each day has to offer us talking to someone you can't see nor hear."

Now I grinned at Pearl, the best friend anyone could ever have. She had pizza sauce above her lip, and she held a ladle. Probably had been using it as a fake microphone before I got here.

"That Buddy," she said right in my ear. "He's hot! Evie, I sure have missed you! I don't ever want to leave for an entire summer again."

Her arms were around me in a hug. The ladle hit me in the hip. She kissed my cheek and set me free. "Oh, why did you have to move? Why do you have to go to a different high school?"

Just like that I was exhausted.

It had been a long day.

One that caused more stress than should be allowed for someone on what was supposed to be the best day of her life.

First a storm, then scaring a huge medium and makeup and hair products and three almost strangers standing in my kitchen chatting. If I could just slink off with Pearl—well, *that* would have been the icing on the cake, no pun intended.

"Let's sneak out of here," Buddy said in my ear. His breath felt like humid storm weather on my neck. My whole body warmed up. I jerked around to see him better.

"For your present," he said. "You know."

Pearl squinched her eyes at Buddy. "I don't think so, Mr. Buddy McKay. Girls all over town know about your wily ways. Evie is going nowhere with you!" She tossed her hair at him and locked elbows with me. Then she giggled. "Go with him. Later," she said where no one else could hear. She giggled again and I was so happy to see Pearl, I thought I might bust wide open, even though I was tired out.

That's what a good best friend does for you. It was nice to see her. Two days before school started. Not perfect, but great.

"Come on, Evie," she said, tugging me by the elbow. Her blond hair, braided and thick as a rope, swung forward when she pulled on my arm. "Let's you and me go get us our signature pizza."

16

When Baby Lucy was asleep and JimDaddy had sung himself hoarse crooning old heartbreaker songs while we danced
in an awkward group of five plus three (and sang along with
JimDaddy, sounding pretty good at times, I must admit) and
Pearl called her momma and argued with her to pleeease let
her stay the night and her momma said no, not with you being
gone for so long, so she had to go home, and everyone else had
left, too, there came a knock at the door.

Aunt Odie.

"Hey," Momma said, kissing at Aunt Odie's face. "What
are you doing here so late? Back for more cake?"

"I need Evie," Aunt Odie said. Her voice was strained.

Ahhhh, here to tell me about her auntie Doris. I wasn't
sure I could handle it right now, though.

She walked into the living room (Aunt Odie, not Auntie
Doris), limping like one leg was four inches shorter than the
other.

Baby Lucy, who awoke for only a few seconds, reached

plump hands toward Aunt Odie, who kissed at the air near her. "Can't right now, honey," she said, and then, "Your room, Evie. And bring a hacksaw."

"What?"

Momma raised her eyebrows.

"I mean scissors."

JimDaddy, who was going around the living room with a huge garbage bag, said, "Going after that mustache of yours, Odie?" He snickered, and his blue eyes twinkled.

Aunt Odie might not have heard him. At least she didn't answer.

I followed her down the hall, remembering Tommie at the last minute. The girl had never come out to the party. Was she still in my room?

Aunt Odie threw the door open and collapsed on my bed. She let out a sigh that might have started a storm if we had been outside. There was no Tommie.

"Shut the door, honey," she said.

I did.

"Lock it." Aunt Odie wiped at her brow. "Bad news," she said. "Bad news!"

My heart jumped like it was trying to climb out of my body. I swallowed twice to keep it down where it should be.

"Aunt Odie, does this have to do with my Gift?"

Aunt Odie pulled her dress up above her knees where I could see the girdle. Flesh poked out of every tiny hole.

It looked like a million little balls of white bread, risen and ready to be thrown in the oven.

"I can't get it off," she said.

All the way up, like a pair of terrible living shorts.

The sight woke me right up.

"Why?" I said. "I mean, what? I mean, how did that happen?"

"Humidity, I am sure," she said with a sniff.

It took me two hours to cut the thing off.

17

It was almost midnight when Aunt Odie, red-faced and no longer limping, left for home.

"Girl," she said when I stood on the porch with her, "I hope you have learned a lesson."

"Ummm," I said.

The moon was fat in the sky, truly made of cheese and close enough to touch. It was the color of a block of cheddar and just as shiny.

She whispered, "Never wear a girdle."

"Yes, ma'am."

"And here's more advice."

I yawned.

"You've never heard me talk about Auntie Doris, not your whole life."

Tree frogs called out in the night. Singing. Begging for more rain.

"Not that I can remember."

Aunt Odie pointed at me. "And here's why. She gave up her last name on her wedding day."

Me and Aunt Odie stood there, eye to eye.

"Accepted the common last name of Smith, and the rest is history."

"She lost her name . . ."

"And her power."

Big deal. I didn't even *get* a power. I didn't dare say those words out loud, though, but so what?

"She could make flowers bloom in midwinter. Then she let some man come in and convince her to change her last name. And take her off to Indiana."

"What does that have to do with my Gift?" I said.

Aunt Odie hesitated. "It was too much for her. A burden."

"Doesn't seem like a burden."

"A professional makes things look easy," Aunt Odie said. "Okay."

She leaned close. "My auntie quit believing in herself. In her abilities."

Behind me, Momma's momma's papa's clock chimed out midnight.

"And her life went from bad to worse."

"What do you mean worse?"

"She lost her happiness. That core what makes a Messenger a Messenger." Aunt Odie put her hand on my shoulder. "We're here to help, dumpling."

I nodded. "I see," I said, though it was like looking through a glass darkly, like the Scriptures say.

"Gotta get," Aunt Odie said with a fresh breath. "See you at the house to help me with a new mix recipe I wanna to try." She got in her car and drove off down the street. I saw her turn into her drive. She waved from her porch, then flashed the light at me.

"Hey, Evie."

I jumped, nearly tearing the door handle off as I went to walk back inside.

"Buddy." My voice was harsh. "What are you doing here?"

"Hush now," he said, stepping out of the the azalea bushes and up onto the porch. "Just making sure you get in your place all right."

I raised my eyebrows at him.

"You look awful . . ." Buddy paused. I heard him swallow from six feet away.

"What?" I said. "Jeez, Buddy, it's my birthday. I don't think you should be saying things like that to the birthday girl."

"I meant," he said, taking in a deep breath, "you look awful pretty, Evie. In this weak light, for a second there, you looked like someone I used to know. Got me a little tongue-tied."

I put a fake smile on my face.

Placed my hands on my hips.

Someone else, huh?

We stood there glaring at each other. At least I was glaring.

"I pitch for our high school baseball team," Buddy said at last. "*Starting* pitcher."

I couldn't think of a thing to say.

He hopped up on the porch with me. "I might play professional ball," he said, taking a step closer. I backed up till I touched the doorknob. "That's the goal. What about you?"

"I'm not that interested in playing baseball," I said.

Buddy dipped his head and laughed. The sound was fat and full. A real laugh. One that woulda made Aunt Odie proud.

He smiled at me.

"That's not all, Evie," Buddy said. "I still want to kiss you."

He looked awful himself, standing in that flood of cheesy moonlight.

"I'm not so sure," I said, swallowing, "that I ought to do that."

In one step he stood next to me. I had to look up to see into his eyes. He put his hands on my shoulders. I could feel his fingers shaking where he touched me.

"You can't turn fifteen," he said, leaning closer, "without a kiss."

I could, I thought. Then I said it out loud. "I could."

A voice in my head, somewhere near my left ear, told me

I was already done turning fifteen. August 25 was over. Had chimed away as I walked Aunt Odie out the door.

How did Buddy smell so good? Not a thing like cake and root beer and ice cream. More like something citrusy. Soapy citrusy.

"I'm gonna do it," he said. Then pressed his lips to mine. Soft, almost not there.

The kiss was finished before it began, almost, and there went Buddy, off across the front yard, leaving his parting path in the dewy grass.

I could see the moon shining on his T-shirt.

Could see the words, LIVING ON A PRAYER, floating away in the dark like a spirit.

18

In my room, long after I was settled under the covers, I thought about Buddy and his kiss, and each time my stomach folded over on itself like I was putting beaten egg white into a batter.

"I should have kissed him, straight up," I said to my darkened room. My eyes grew heavy.

A breeze, light as a breath, moved the curtains. Pushed them away from the window like someone wanted to sneak in.

It had been a good day.

A long day.

A tiring day.

With Aunt Odie starting and almost ending it.

My aunt.

Who took care of us.

Then when me and Momma moved in with JimDaddy, Aunt Odie bought the first house that went up for sale on the street and moved there.

My aunt close.

Too sleepy to open my eyes.

Her auntie Doris no longer a Messenger.

Sounds from down the hall.

In Indiana where maybe no one believed in the dead helping you out.

And JimDaddy melancholy all the time. I didn't know that till right now. And Baby Lucy. And my daddy died when I was just two and Momma and me with Aunt Odie till Momma met up again with my stepfather on a dating website and there was a light in the room. Bouncing, fluttering like Tinker Bell. Pausing at the closet. Moving close to where I lay in bed. Right by my face.

Then.

Sleep.

And

that

low

cry

sad enough to peel paint off the walls.

19

"Here I am," she says.
And if I weren't so tired, I'd answer.
"Right here."

20

"What took you so long?" My aunt rested a hand on her hip and stared out at me.

"Do you have to do it through the screen door? Let me in," I said. "It's hot as fire out here."

"What do you expect when you sleep till noon in the South?"

"Air-conditioning," I said, and pushed past Aunt Odie.

I headed toward the room Aunt Odie had built into a specialty kitchen, walking the long way through a large living room and then the enormous dining room. Everything was cool in here. Cool and clean and ready for us to get to working. My face was a blur in the stainless double-door fridge.

Ingredients were spread out on the counter. A bag of flour. A half-dozen pale-pink eggs. Cream. Milk. Butter. Spices like curry and cinnamon and cardamom.

"Sit, please, Evie."

I flapped my T-shirt against my body some, letting the cool air of the house dry me off a little.

That's how hot it is in Florida in August. Go on a hike just eight houses down the street and you had to shower again. My hair was still straight on accounta Aunt Carol's Gift. Plus, I still had on a glimmer of eye shadow. But neither of those things helped with the heat.

"Yes, ma'am." I sat on the stool and swiveled this way and that while Aunt Odie lowered herself onto her own stool.

"How're you feeling since the girdle incident?" I asked.

"Bumpy still." Aunt Odie hiked at her dress a little. "Wanna see? I even got bruises. . . ."

I shook my head. "I believe you. No need in proving it."

Aunt Odie let her dress drop, then took my hands in both of hers. "The living," she said, "ain't far from the dead."

I glanced around the room. I couldn't see anyone . . . lingering.

"The veil between our world and theirs is thin. Keep that in mind. Always."

"Okay."

"It's easy to slip up with the dead," Aunt Odie. Her face was so serious I couldn't look away even though I wanted to. "You wanna end up like my auntie?"

I shook my head.

"Good. Now, first things first," she said. "Anything happen last night?"

My cheeks turned warm. "I . . ." Should I tell her about the kiss—though it was barely a kiss—before I told my very own momma what had happened? I couldn't see Momma liking what I had done at all.

"Well . . ."

"Any visions? Burning bushes? Voices?"

I let out air I didn't know I had been holding.

That. Oh.

"No, Aunt Odie," I said. "Nothing."

She nodded. Tapped her finger against her lips. There was a flour handprint on her apron. I hoped it was her own. "But," she said, almost to herself, like she was thinking so hard she had forgotten I was in the room, "but it was a full-moon night. I know she's the right one. It couldn't be the baby. I dreamed *Evie*."

Who was she talking to?

"Aunt Odie?"

She looked at me and I saw her see me. "Nothing out of the ordinary?"

"No, ma'am."

Except for my first kiss.

I smiled politely.

My stomach folded over.

Aunt Odie leaned close to me so that she tipped on two legs of her stool. "Something's different about you." She let all four stool legs, plus her own two feet, rest on the floor.

I glanced at the ingredients. Back at her.

"Should I . . ." I said. Then stopped. Could Aunt Odie see,

if she walked all the way around viewing my whole body, that I had let Buddy kiss me? Could she see I had wanted him to do it again? And again?

Now Aunt Odie stood and went to the counter. She plucked up a recipe card. I could see the ink from here. It looked like the kind that came from a calligraphy pen. I imagined that ghosty hand, writing.

"So what are we working on today?" I asked. My voice sounded wimpy. Scared. Even I heard that. "You said something about getting a new recipe you wanted to try?"

"No," Aunt Odie said. "What's going on with you?" She was back again. Walking around me as best she could, considering I was slid up close to the table, looking me over from top to bottom, sliding my stool out so she could circle me—and give me a thorough once-over.

Did the Gift leave a mark? I sure hoped not.

Did kisses?

She put her face close to mine.

"Something is going on," she said. Her voice was church-toned.

I pretended to look her in the eye but stared at the bridge of her nose instead.

And I kept my lips tight, no matter how she questioned. Then we set to working on a new Bundt cake recipe that tasted so good, once it was mixed and baked (with love), I wanted to cry.

21

Aunt Odie and I worked all afternoon.

Stirring, sifting, baking, adding ingredients ("Not everything comes perfect from the dead. Adjustments must be made."), baking some more. Pouring, measuring, mixing. Baking even more. Tasting, scraping, and at last, at last her saying, "Done!" with a smack of her lips.

"We'll get this on the market after all the approvals are met." Aunt Odie looked sort of business-y now. Even though her hair fought to get out from under a hairnet and she'd splattered flour all over when she opened the bag. "Our job is to perfect, considering what we have been given. I wouldn't do anything less."

During a break, I stood at the front door watching Buddy's house.

Heat shimmered off the blacktop. When a car drove through or someone walked down the street, they looked like part of a mirage.

I took a deep breath.

"You sure there wasn't something?" Aunt Odie asked my back.

What did ghosts whisper? Tattletale things? I didn't dare look at my aunt. A feather of a kiss changes a girl. I knew that now.

"I'm sure," I said. Relieved and not.

And Aunt Odie said under her breath, "I will be cat-kicked."

22

It felt like my skin was getting a good steaming when I stepped outside.

I carried Aunt Odie's newest creation. Almond Bundt cake with vanilla icing. Crispy. Buttery. Just the right amount of sweet.

Made with love.

"So you see a ghost?" I had asked her.

"No."

"Does one help you measure the ingredients?"

"Don't make fun now, honey. You know they don't. *You* do."

"I'm not making fun," I had said, and ran a knife across a full cup of flour, making it smooth. Flour needs to be exact.

Aunt Odie had set aside the sifter. "It happens between being awake and going to sleep. That's when I see it. But not always." She raised a finger to me. "I have to be worthy. I have to have made the best of the last recipe. I've learned that over the years. So the recipes come in waves. Sometimes nothing. Then, when I have made the most of the last gift, that blank three-by-five. A hand—it looks different every time, I'm guessing because it's a new person with a recipe—writes out the words." She raised her other pointer finger at me. "And, voilà!"

Only she said it *Vo-la*.

Now I stepped on the porch, remembering.

Seemed like a lot of work for getting a new recipe. Of course, sometimes you have to work for a Gift. Momma and Aunt Odie and the rest of the Messengers all say that.

Sheesh.

It's a Gift, I thought, walking home. *Something should be easy about a Gift*.

Heat rose off the street. Did I look like a mirage going in the middle of the road carrying a delicious Bundt cake like this? The light scent of vanilla floated around me.

Eight houses down and I was home.

"Momma?" I called when I got inside.

The place was silent.

A note waited for me on the kitchen table. I set Aunt Odie's newest creation down and read,

> Off with Baby Lucy.
> Someone called for you.
> I gave him your number.
> Be back after the show.

Him?

My heart pitter-pattered.

I opened the fridge, pulled out the OJ, and drank from the pitcher. Momma couldn't stop me, seeing she wasn't here. I patted my hip pocket. Where was my phone?

I pulled off my dirty-slash-sweaty T-shirt and headed down the hall toward the laundry room.

Stripped off my shorts and underclothing. Hurried to my bedroom, cooling off with the AC and my nakedness.

In my room, I pulled new stuff outta the dresser. (Oh, there it was. My phone sat next to the mirror. I'd forgotten to take it. And it looked like I had four text messages and had even missed a few phone calls. I would shower, then check.)

Did Buddy call? I thought as I stepped into the lukewarm water.

Soaped up.

Rinsed off.

Thought of that ghostlike kiss on my lips.

Dried off.

Got dressed and walked right back to where Tommie sat on the edge of my bed.

23

I let out a scream that could have shattered glass.

Nope, the mirror was still intact. Window, too.

"What are you doing in here?" I asked, covering my breasts, though I was dressed.

"Nothing you wouldn't do," Tommie said.

"Excuse me?" I stood in the doorway, staring at her. Was she still crying? Well, I didn't care. You don't just barge into someone's room. . . . Hold on. "How do you keep getting in here?"

She rolled her eyes. She was acting awful snooty, seeing she was in my house. "Through the back. You know you can jimmy the lock coming into the laundry room."

"No, I didn't."

"Now you do."

We stared at each other. For a moment I didn't know how to answer. I was too surprised for words.

"I like the color in here," Tommie said.

"This tired color? Whatever. Thanks. I think. Considering you shouldn't be here."

We stood a moment longer.

"You have to leave," came out of my mouth without me thinking the words, but I knew they were right once I heard them. "You can call me on my new phone, if you want. I'll text you the number. But you can't just show up unannounced like this."

She was frail, I saw. Almost not there. Pretty but young looking. And looking at her face, I was certain she'd been crying. "No need to show me out," she said, and was down the hall before I could turn. I heard the door slam behind her.

I followed.

The frilly curtains that covered the glass on the back door—a touch Momma added when we got here—trembled.

I checked the knob. It jiggled in my hand, loose. Why was I shaking?

Then I went to Momma's note. Reread it.

How long till the movie was done? And where was Jim-Daddy? Usually they went together, no matter when Momma wanted to go, no matter the show. Seeing *Slam Ball Heartbreak* was their first date. They've kept up the tradition.

Now my heart was in my throat. Why weren't they together?

I made sure the door was locked—it was—then headed to my bedroom as the front doorbell rang.

24

A burst of annoyance flared through me. I would tell Tommie not to show up again. To call, like I said. Not just traipse around to the front door and ring the bell. Tommie scared me, coming in like that. For all I knew, she could have had a gun. Or a knife. All I had was a cake, a dense cake, yes, but I hadn't ever heard of anyone stopping a murderer with a food product.

The doorbell sounded again.

I pattered to the front room. I would tell her to meet me at school. "She has to live near," I said. Right? Or had she slept outside? How long had she been in the house? My blood rattled through me.

"Maybe I should have spoken to her longer," I said. I couldn't bring myself to be mean to her. She was upset. That much was clear. "I should have just talked to her."

Fine! I'd talk to her! See what she was worried over.

I peered through the glass. Fell back against the wall.

Buddy!

25

"I saw you," Buddy said. "Evie, I saw you look out at me."

"No, you didn't."

There was silence. "Yes . . . I did."

"I know that," I said. Still I leaned against the wall, my head brushing up against a family photo in a frame that said FAMILIES ARE FOREVER. And knowing the things I was learning daily about ghosts and recipes and Bundt cakes, it seemed this saying was more true than I'd thought.

"Hello?" Buddy tapped on the leaded glass of the front door.

My heart beat so hard I thought I might puke. Happy heart beating, yes. And happy puking, too. Throw-up, though, could be a turnoff.

"What do you want, Buddy?"

"Let me in."

"I can't," I said. "Momma and JimDaddy are gone. And so's the baby." I was smiling. Huge, huge smiling. I had forgotten about Tommie. No, I hadn't. Jeez. I was thinking of her right this moment while Buddy stood on my front porch.

"You didn't call me back."

"I haven't had the chance."

"You have. I seen you come home."

What? Both Buddy *and* Tommie watching and waiting for me?

Did he know about the back door?

"Do *you* know about my back door?" I said.

"How you can jimmy it? Yes, I do. But I am not a trespasser. Let me in, Evie." His voice had dropped down to almost nothing. I was surprised I could hear his words at all. "I come to finish what I started last night."

"Excuse me?" My face warmed up. My smile grew.

"The kiss. It wasn't any good at all. I shoulda . . . I shoulda . . ."

I opened the door and Buddy fell into the room, catching himself against me.

He had me by the shoulders. His fingers so warm. I looked into his eyes. Those nut-colored eyes. Pecans. "You know," I said, after swallowing three times, "I'm not allowed to have boys in my house while Momma and JimDaddy are gone." I shut the door closed and turned the dead bolt, locking us both in.

Buddy nodded. "I know Jimmy's rules," he said. His voice was a whisper. "But I been thinking about you all night, Evie." He slid his hands down my arms. Caught my fingertips with his. "How I shoulda held you longer." He stepped nearer, pulling my arm around his waist. Circled my own waist, pressing into the small of my back. "And really looked at you."

"It was dark," I said. I was whispering too.

He closed his eyes. "And then . . ."

I stood on tiptoe to meet his lips.

"Your hair's wet," he said. His hand in my hair. He was a fast mover.

I nodded.

"I shoulda done all that," Buddy said.

Someone knocked.

Buddy started.

"Kiss me," I said.

"There's not enough time now," he said. Then he walked into the living room and flopped down on the sofa while I threw back the latch and opened the door to Aunt Odie.

26

"Just as I thought," she said.

Aunt Odie looked from me to Buddy to me again. She had a bit of tobacco on her lip. Must have gotten a smoke on her ride down. I glanced out the window. Yup. There was the Cadillac. "I knew something had changed. Saw it when you come in this morning."

"You're"—Aunt Odie pointed at Buddy—"as shifty-eyed as a Bible salesman."

"I don't even read the Bible," Buddy said. *He* looked a little green around the gills.

"Not the right thing to say," Aunt Odie said. She came into the living room and sat in a wingback chair.

"Ummm," Buddy said. He sort of stood.

"Sit," Aunt Odie said.

Oh. No.

Down Buddy went.

"There aren't Bible salesmen anymore, Aunt Odie," I said with a sigh.

Buddy stared at me. Then nodded. Then shook his head no. At last he shrugged.

"Your momma," Aunt Odie said, "won't stand for any of this nonsense." She pointed between the two of us.

"Aunt Odie," I said, "there hasn't been time for nonsense. And what do you mean by that anyway?" I raised my eyebrows. Tilted my head in the direction of the door.

She'd brought the smell of home cooking with her, and my mouth watered. Not sure if that was because of a yummy dinner (though I was still full from our work together) or because of a yummy Buddy.

Aunt Odie said, "Messengers are"—she paused—"sensitive women."

"I believe that," Buddy said. He sat forward in his chair, hands clasped before him.

"Do you?" Aunt Odie asked.

"Yes, I do." His smile was so sincere my breath caught in my throat.

Things were getting serious. I needed her to leave. I signaled with my eyes for her to go. Gestured with my head toward the door. Aunt Odie folded her arms across her stomach. Dang it! She wasn't going anywhere. No! She was settling in.

"We're newish to the neighborhood," Aunt Odie said to Buddy.

He nodded.

"I been here less than a year."

He nodded again.

"What about you?"

Buddy cleared his throat. "All my life. I was born at Fish Memorial."

Now Aunt Odie nodded.

"What more can you tell me about you, Buddy?"

This was Aunt Odie gearing up for a holdout. I sighed.

She turned to me. "Now, Evie," she said. "Don't be rude. You got something to offer our guest?"

Sheesh.

"I do," I said. "Buddy, you want some homemade Bundt cake? It's still warm."

Buddy perked up. "Thought it smelled sweet in here." He gave me a meaningful look.

I blushed.

He said, "If you don't mind."

I didn't.

"Me too, Evie," Aunt Odie said. "If'n you don't mind."

I minded.

"All righty then," I said, and hotfooted it into the kitchen. I kept one ear aimed in their direction, but they were too far away. Their voices echoed on the marble floor, making the sounds blurry. I hurried to slice the cake, drizzle a bit more icing on top, pull out a sliced strawberry for decoration, pour a glass of OJ for them both (what they didn't know about me drinking from the container wouldn't hurt them), put everything on a tray, and walk it on back to the front room.

"I, um, I want to be lawyer," Buddy was saying. He looked more relaxed. "Like my dad. Maybe open a practice of my own. Or join up with him."

I handed Buddy a plate and drink, then walked Aunt Odie her dessert over. I wasn't sure how she could eat another bite, seeing how we had baked and cooked and mixed and tasted for hours that morning. But that's the thing about Aunt Carolina's recipes (made with love). There's a dash of something heavenly in them that makes you want to keep eating. Even if you are the creator. Or her niece.

Get. On. Outta. Here. Get. On. Out.

I sat on the sofa just down from Buddy, not quite close enough to touch him unless Aunt Odie looked away. Which she didn't. Every time she glanced at me, I sent her silent Morse code.

She ignored me.

"And? What kind of grades you earn?"

That didn't seem fair, seeing as Aunt Odie didn't have any degree at all. Not even one from high school.

"All A's, ma'am," Buddy said, and he smiled when he said it. His teeth were as white as Betty Crocker vanilla icing.

Outside a car screamed past, and a neighbor yelled for the driver to slow down. The sun headed toward bed. The air conditioner kicked on.

"You're proud of that, aren't you?"

"Yes, ma'am, I am."

Aunt Odie looked at me. "Go get me another drink, honey. Get another for Buddy, too. Make us a mint julep this time. There should be a mix in your refrigerator. Brought it over for your momma last week."

"With bourbon or without?"

She paused. Like she was thinking. "Without."

I stood. "If this isn't some kinda ploy to get me outta here," I said. I gave Aunt Odie the evil eye.

"Yes, it is," Aunt Odie said.

"I can help you," Buddy said, standing, his plate and glass in both hands.

"No, you won't. This here interview isn't done."

That *interview* went on for another thirty-eight minutes, until Momma and Baby Lucy pulled in the drive and Buddy excused himself with a "See ya, Evie" and ran out the back door, the same way Tommie (who I *did* forget about) went.

27

"I like him," Aunt Odie said, and swallowed down her third mint julep. "What about you? Now I need to visit the little girls' room."

I had just enough time to think *Do I?* before Momma handed me Baby Lucy.

"Where's JimDaddy?" I asked.

Aunt Odie stood near the chair.

I plopped Baby Lucy onto my lap. She was falling asleep in my arms.

"Off," Momma said, and she wouldn't look neither me nor Aunt Odie straight on. Instead she stomped down the hall. I heard her bedroom door slam closed.

"What's that all about?" Aunt Odie asked.

I shrugged.

"Better potty, then go see."

In her bedroom, I changed my baby sister, put her down with her pacifier, and whispered, "What do I think of Buddy?"

Baby Lucy didn't say anything. She was dead asleep now.

I patted her little belly.

There was plenty of time to find out.

28

She's in between rooms.
In the walls.
Up and down the halls.
Busy all night.

29

The chance didn't happen that day. Or the next.

And, just like I knew it would, school starting got closer. Momma had me out and about, trying to get ready.

To Aunt Carol's shop so she could teach me a thing or two about my hair.

Down to Penney's to shop for school clothes. And Wet Seal with my gift card.

Took me to the hardware store for paint so we could put a fresh new aqua color on my room. "For a whole new start," she said.

"Shoulda done this during the summer," I said once we had covered one wall. I had paint splattered up and down my arms.

Momma, with Baby Lucy hitched to her chest in a baby carrier, said, "You know I was too pregnant for any of that."

I laughed. "Momma, you weren't pregnant at all. Lucy is going on nine months old."

Lucy looked at me. There was paint on one cheek and in

her hair. It was clear me and Momma didn't have a decorating Gift.

Momma smiled. I had to admit she looked good since this baby. Since JimDaddy. Not that living with Aunt Odie had been bad.

"A new baby on the outside is harder than a baby on the inside, you know." Momma edged up near the ceiling, painting a perfect line. She stopped long enough to kiss Lucy, who sucked on her bottom lip. Then Momma said, "Look at us here, Evie. A brand-new family made up of two broken families. Love's made us whole."

"Yes, ma'am," I said. My thoughts flicked to Buddy. To the butterfly kiss. To his soapy smell.

"I never thought I would find me another one to try and love," she said. She stepped down off the chair we had found in the garage. "Not after your daddy passed on. But honey, I did."

"Yes, ma'am."

"And you will too." When she looked at me, I saw worry in her eyes.

"What?" I said.

"What what?" she said back. Then she said again, "Yes sirree. You're gonna find yourself your own love."

Um. Wait a minute. I didn't say anything. Just painted. Was that worried look for me? Or about what I might do?

"Have you already?"

I didn't even slow the roller. "You been talking to Aunt Odie?"

"Maybe."

Momma came to stand next to me. I was surprised to see I could look her right in the eye. Why, I was as tall as my mother. When had that happened? On my birthday?

"You got anything to say?"

I shook my head. Dipped at the paint again. "Not yet," I said.

Momma leaned so close I could smell milk on Lucy's breath. "You know I love you most of all, right?"

I set the roller down into the pan. Planted a kiss on Momma's face.

"I do," I said. "And I love you most of all too."

30

What more could a girl want than a new coat of paint? A momma and aunts and a stepdaddy and a baby sister who loved her most of all?

Not including a good make-out session.

Nothing.

Not one more thing.

31

When Tuesday, August 28 rolled around, I was up extra early, ready. The sun hadn't even peeked an eye over the horizon. The house was quiet. Smelled of magnolias.

I had my hair braided (all Aunt Carol's good-luck hair technique had gotten caught in the crazy curls the night before, so I'd braided the mess). After several more minutes deliberating, I chose just-the-right-length shorts and a pink-sprinkle-colored top and pulled them on.

Then I sat on the edge of my bed and spent a good fifteen minutes looking at myself in the mirror. Batting my eyes. Behind me, a wisp of white moved. I turned. Glanced around the room. Let out a sigh. This place looked good aqua.

After a while, I slipped down the hall and went on in the kitchen. The coffeepot was on and the red light gleamed in the reflection of the marble countertop. I preheated the oven. Sat to think at the bar.

"This place," I said. "Ooooeee!" All reverence and thankfulness.

This home didn't compare at all to our old trailer out on Mission Road. Some of that had been tough years if all you're considering is money. When Aunt Odie couldn't stand it anymore, she took us in. She was moving up in the mixes business world. Starting to haul in cash.

I sighed, remembering.

True love for Momma, and a perfect house for all, because of a reconnection on a lovey-dovey website. I was still amazed by it.

And maybe there would be some good kisses for me, too. My face heated up at the thought.

"Get going, Evie," I said. Outside, the oaks didn't wave a leaf. The yard was still.

I popped the Aunt Carolina's rise-in-the-fridge rolls into the oven and pulled out a couple of eggs, compliments of Nina, Pinta, or Santa Maria, the shells blushing.

"Thank you, girls," I said, hoping my words would carry off down the street to where they roosted. After a few minutes, breakfast was done, and I took a tray in to Momma, who slept on her stomach, her hair as big as a fan.

"Momma?" I said. "You awake?"

"No more crying," she said, her voice clear and loud. I looked around the room.

"You're talking in your sleep," I whispered, jiggling the bed with my knee. "I gotta go to school soon, and I brought you a surprise." The egg yolks trembled.

My mother rolled over to look at me. "Evie?"

"Yes, ma'am."

She looked so young. And sad. This morning she was sad.

"Is that you?"

"Yes, ma'am."

She sat up a little. "I thought . . ." Momma stretched some. "I thought you were someone else."

"Who's that? A famous movie star?"

Momma propped herself up in bed, then pulled the sheet over her tummy. Her giant T-shirt nightgown sagged at the neck.

"I'm not so sure. A girl. A coupl'a years younger than you are. I thought you were her. I keep dreaming she's watching me."

A chill ran down my arms.

"What's all this for?" Momma stretched again and smiled.

JimDaddy's side of the bed was empty. He has to drive into Orlando, where he's doing some building. He leaves every morning by five forty-five. Always gets the coffee going for Momma.

"One of the things that made me love him," Momma has said. "He might not sleep long at night, but he makes sure to get the coffee percolating."

Momma also says JimDaddy is the best builder this side of the Mississippi. I don't know if that's true or not.

I sat on the edge of the bed, still holding the tray. "I won't be here today. Not to help you. I thought this would be a nice way for you to start the school year."

Momma smiled so big her eyes went squinty. "Thank you, Evie. You are so thoughtful. Though shouldn't I be doing that for you?"

I handed the food over to Momma. She ate, taking big bites. I nibbled at my own food. My stomach was nervous.

"You know, Evie," she said. "You got Aunt Odie's gift for cooking, that's for sure." She sopped at an egg with a buttered roll.

"Think so?"

I thought of Aunt Odie getting recipes from her dreams and ghostly hands. "She's teaching me everything she knows," I said. "To pass on the business, I think."

"That something you want to do? Carry on the Aunt Carolina tradition?"

I shrugged. "Maybe. I love to cook."

"She always did like you best," Momma said, nodding. "And I do too."

Momma says this to Baby Lucy, too.

32

I was halfway down the street (I saw no hint of Tommie. Where had she got to?) when Buddy pulled up alongside me in his family's car.

"You need a ride, Evie?" he said.

The morning was beautiful. The air not too humid. The smell of the ocean rolling into this side of town. A mockingbird cried out from across the street. Here, periwinkles were tucked under the oak trees. They nodded as I passed.

I shook my head. "I don't think so, Buddy," I said, making sure I didn't look him in the eye. That would be my undoing. "I told my momma I wanted to walk. It's too pretty a day to be in a"—I glanced at the vehicle—"van."

"You want I should park this thing and walk with you?" Buddy hung out the window, almost not looking at the way he was going. "I will," he said. "I'll put this thing in park and leave it right here. If you want."

The school bus zoomed past, riffling my clothes. Someone hollered out the window and a 7-Eleven cup exploded a few feet up the road from me. I patted at my braid. Smoothed down the new shirt Momma had given me after breakfast. No sprinkles after all.

"That's okay," I said.

But Buddy wasn't listening. He pulled the van over, parking not too far from the fire station.

"My uncle works there," I heard him say as the driver's-side window went up.

Buddy popped out of the car. Slammed the door behind him.

Now the sun painted streaks of yellow across the sky. In fact, the whole morning reminded me of that yolk Momma had eaten, the way she swirled it over her plate.

Buddy slid up next to me.

"I shaved," he said.

My mouth went dry.

"That's an odd thing to say," I said. His skin did look smooth. For a moment I wanted to stand on my tiptoes and put my nose in his neck.

"I knew someone who liked it when—"

Nope. Didn't want to hear about it. "I see."

We walked the rest of the way to school, quiet, his fingers brushing against mine every once in a while, making my heart thrum like the whirring of a hand mixer.

33

So high school.

Tenth grade.

Lots of kids.

Too many fluorescent lights. Too many slamming lockers. Not enough privacy.

Stinky people. Teeth too white. And no one with hair as big as mine. (Thank goodness most of it was tied into submission.)

I didn't have one class with Pearl because she went to the school on the other side of town (boo!). I didn't see Vera or Julius, either. But this place crawled with people. All sizes. All colors. All temperaments.

Gosh, I felt lonely. And in this crowd.

"Rather be at home," I said to myself as I sat in my first class, trying to get used to taking notes again. Tears blurred my eyes. I sniffed and waited for the hours to pass so I could get on home.

When I hurried out of algebra, three people running into

me with not so much as a pardon me, though, there stood Buddy.

"Hey, Evie," he said.

The walls echoed with noise, but I couldn't help but smile. "Hey." I dabbed at my eyes with the back of my hand.

"Walk you to your next class?"

"Sure. Yes. Thank you."

Going down the hallway—the too-bright, too-loud, too-lonely hallway—with someone, I didn't feel so neglected.

A girl I didn't know ran up to Buddy and threw herself into his arms. She kissed his face.

"Kelly," Buddy said, looking down at her. "Have a good summer?"

"Yes." She pouted at him. I noticed her hair was perfect, both calm *and* silky. "Didn't see you, though." She poked him in the chest. I couldn't see any Bundt cake ingredients under her nails. Not that I had any. I'd showered, after all. Several times since the Bundt cake incident.

"Busy," Buddy said. He looked over at me.

She did too. Then she raised her chin and faced him again.

"A sophomore, Buddy?" she asked. Then, "See you after school."

"Maybe," he said.

We hurried on. The second bell rang as we got to my classroom. The next one would be the late bell.

"She isn't anyone to me now," Buddy said. "That girl. She was a rebound. You know?"

"No." I shrugged. I did feel a little steamed. "This sophomore doesn't really care," I said. But I did care.

"I'll walk you to your desk," Buddy said. "Where you want to sit?"

I pointed to a chair next to a window, three back to the left. Now, if I needed to, I could look out at the sky and the palm trees. If we opened a window, maybe the smell of magnolias would float through on a mellow breeze.

Me and Buddy went across the room, winding between chairs. Until at last he said, "See ya, Evie. You know I can walk you to class anytime."

I settled my backpack on the floor next to my desk. When I looked up, Buddy had moved closer to me.

Kissing in school?

"Thank you," I said, and stuck my hand out.

He pulled back, gave me a solemn look, then shook my hand.

"Hey, McKay!" A guy at the back of the room gallumped to where we stood. "I thought they kicked you outta school for good."

Buddy slapped hands with this guy, who wore basketball shorts and untied Nikes.

"Finished my parole," Buddy said. He turned to me. "Don't tell your aunt I said that."

I sat down. "Okay."

Looked to the window.

So. My love life with Buddy was over before it began. Parole wouldn't sit well with anyone in my family.

The teacher walked in just as Buddy and Nikes Guy bumped shoulders and slapped hands again. It was like watching a sitcom.

A breeze moved the palm tree branches. Maybe a typhoon would hit and interrupt . . .

The late bell rang and the teacher said, "All y'all take a seat."

Buddy leaned over me. "See ya later, Evie." He left the room, running into two desks as he went out.

Well, maybe the romance was back on. If I could forgive the rebound with the great hair.

34

No baby snuggles.

    No eating in front of the television.

    No mixing and laughing and just being.

    No Messengers.

35

What about me?

36

Buddy met me at the end of school.

I felt as worn out as an old rag used to scrub one of Aunt Odie's six-burner gas ranges (she has two).

"Rough day?" he said.

"Long." I let out a sigh.

"Think you can make it all the way back home? It's a good mile plus." Buddy took my backpack from me and slung it over his shoulder. "Or I could ask Hall to drive us. He's the guy in your class."

Which one? I could hardly remember the day. Too much stimulation.

I shook my head no. I could feel the hair escaping from the braid. Even *it* was tired and wanted to be free. Who was it that came up with public schooling anyway? A momma with ten kids who needed free time?

"I'll get better as soon as we get away from here," I said. "But I need to stop at a restroom."

"Sure."

All around us lockers slammed. The floor, clean when I arrived this morning, was gritty like everyone had come in from the beach. There were black scrape marks, and papers littered the tiles. A math book had fallen open to chapter 46 right near a class.

Someone whistled far too loud just as I slipped into the bathroom. I would have taken a deep breath, out of plain exhaustion, but who wants to do that in a bathroom used by too many girls?

As I washed my hands, Tommie stepped out of a stall.

"Oh," she said, sniffing. "It's you."

I stared at her in the mirror. Her hair was smooth and as tired-looking as my hair felt.

"Hello?" I said. Miss Tommie sure was acting high-and-mighty. "That's what real Southern people say when they meet in the restroom."

"Whatever."

I dried off under the hot-air dryer and rolled my eyes. This was the girl who let herself into *my* bedroom *and* house, and she spoke to me like I had done something wrong. Sheesh.

Tommie waved a hand under the automatic water spigot. Nothing happened. "I can never get this to work," she said.

Probably 'cause you're acting ugly, I wanted to say, but Tommie sounded near to weeping, and seeing how I knew how *I* felt at the end of the day, I couldn't help but feel sorry for her. Even if she was a crybaby.

I waved at the faucet, turning the water on for her.

"Why are you mad at me?" I said.

But Tommie didn't answer. Just rubbed her palms together until the water turned off.

She stepped up next to me, drying her hands with me.

"I can't talk about it, really," she said. She looked me right in the eye.

I almost gasped when I saw the pain there. I swallowed.

Tommie swallowed too. Then she said, "I feel like you're taking over my life."

And without another word she walked from the bathroom with three other girls, who had stared at me as though *I* was the weirdo.

"What?" I said, but no one answered.

37

Buddy was just too good-looking for words.

The high school was on the edge of town, and that meant walking down a few roads where there were no sidewalks, just bull anthills and palmetto bushes and lots of sand, too.

"You tired yet, Evie?" he asked every few feet.

"Naw," I said. "I'm good."

Fresh air really did help. Sorta kept me from thinking about Tommie and classes and dumb homework (already!).

The almost last of late August can be an okay time of year to take a hike down the road with a pretty boy, even if school preceded the event.

Buddy carried my bag, talked about guys who are on the baseball team with him, and even said his favorite books were *The Book Thief* and *Feed*.

"Those are awful different," I said.

"Both classics," he said. "Anyway, reading's good for you. Especially if you're a guy." He hesitated. "But don't tell anyone I said that."

"I won't," I said, slipping a little over the crush line.

Not only was he nice. *And* a reader. But he was also a gentleman. A true Southerner. Something Momma said about JimDaddy, and how there didn't seem to be men like this anymore. Buddy walked closest to the road, held my hand every time we started to cross a street, and insisted I walk in whatever shade there was.

At last we arrived to his van.

"Wanna keep walking, or should we get the AC cranked up?" he asked. The sun was frying-pan hot. Too bright. One car passed and then another. The air smelled of the ocean mixed with exhaust.

"We can drive," I said. "If you want."

Buddy drove me home, jumped out of his side of the car and ran to mine, threw open my door, and there, in broad daylight, kissed me. Right on the mouth.

I forgot all about the humidity and a few other things I can't remember.

"I been thinking about that. . . ."

"Yoo-hoo!" It was Aunt Odie, calling from down the street. "Bring that boy down here to talk to me again." No answer from me or Buddy. "I see you two," Aunt Odie hollered, like she needed information.

Buddy kissed me again.

I touched his face. His skin was hot. He tasted like Doublemint gum. Still smelled of soap.

Watson Steinbeck, who lives in the brick house three places down from us, on the same side of the road as me and Aunt Odie, hollered out, "Well, Odie, that there is Buddy McKay."

"I know who it is," Aunt Odie said. "I need to finish my interview with that young man." Her voice sounded screechy.

No, they both did.

I expected Aunt Odie to drive her way down to us. Or maybe even *walk* to where we kissed. Whew! That would be a miracle. And frightening.

I didn't end my kiss just 'cause of that, though. And neither did Buddy. We had another three good smooches.

"Oh, Evie," Buddy said, when he finally pulled away. Then, "We better get down to see what Miss Odie wants. She's gonna tan my hide if we don't."

I didn't say anything. I couldn't talk. Just touch my lips with my fingertips.

We walked down the street, Buddy saying the whole way, "Sure wish you would let me hold your hand."

And me not allowing it because I knew how strong Aunt Odie is. Haven't I seen her working a rolling pin?

"I'd be a whole lot less nervous," Buddy said, leaning over me.

When I looked up at him, the sun winked at me and I was blind for a moment.

You are taking over my life. That Tommie. That Tommie. I squeezed my eyes shut.

What was she doing in my thoughts right now?

Five hundred feet away I saw that Aunt Odie had her arms folded across her bosom. She wore an apron (she almost always does), which she flapped as we got closer. Flour rose in the air around her, and I wondered if maybe, maybe she'd disappear.

She didn't.

"Hello there, young man," Aunt Odie said. She nodded at me. "Evie." Then she stepped out to meet us, letting the door to her screened-in porch slam shut behind her. Aunt Odie reached for Buddy's hand. "Nice to see you again, Buddy."

She smelled like cloves.

Buddy grabbed for me as he reached for Aunt Odie, and I dodged him. No way would I seal his fate.

Not till I had kissed him another few times. Was that selfish?

"Feel like staying for an afternoon snack, young man?"

I saw the words roll through Buddy's head.

More interrogation.

Something delicious to eat.

Buddy walked up the steps. Aunt Odie opened the door wide, where the smell of cloves and cinnamon seemed like a comforter and maybe, maybe we were lured into her house against our will, like children in a fairy tale.

38

We ate raspberry beignets drowned in a vanilla sauce sweet enough to set your teeth on edge. Aunt Odie poured us each two glasses of milk that were so cold I coughed.

Then the timer went off and Aunt Odie brought in plates piled high with . . .

"What is this?" I asked as she handed me a fork and my dish.

"I'm planning on expanding from dry ingredient products that might use eggs, butter, and water." My aunt raised an eyebrow at me. "Thinking of expanding into the freezer section."

I blinked. "You kidding me?"

Aunt Odie smiled. "Didn't sleep so good last night," she said. She settled in her chair.

A ghostly appearance of another recipe! Well, well, well.

"This one has chicken and veggies added. What do you two think?"

Buddy gave Aunt Odie a thumbs-up, and we ate till I thought I might pop. It was so tasty I almost forgot about kissing the cutest boy in the neighborhood. Maybe the cutest boy in the school.

I said I *almost* forgot.

39

Tommie was in my room when I got home.

"Look," she said, when I threw my backpack on the bed. She came at me from behind my open door, surprising me. "We gotta talk."

I clutched at my chest.

Swallowed a scream.

My heart hammered at my ribs, knocking to get free. "Does my momma know you're in here?" I asked. "Did she let you in?"

"I told you," Tommie said, and she settled on the bed, making herself comfortable. "I told you the back latch can be jiggled this way and that and I can get in here on my own."

I shut the bedroom door so Momma, who was putting Baby Lucy down for a nap, wouldn't hear me. "You can't do that."

"It's easy," Tommie said.

"No," I said. My blood was just-like-that at full boil. "It's wrong. Against the law."

"How do you figure?" Tommie's hair was not mussed at

all. I patted at my own head, felt the tangles and craziness, then dropped my hand.

I stepped close to her. So close I could smell something on her. Something I didn't recognize. Something that wasn't exactly pleasant. I took a step back.

"This." I waved my hands, pointing at the room. The new paint job, I could see when I took a closer look, had traces of pale pink coming through. How could that be? Me and Momma had put on a primer first. Sherwin-Williams had a thing or two to explain. I kept waving. "This is my room."

Tommie, who had been pushing at her cuticles, looked at me. Startled, I'd say.

"No, it isn't," she said.

I sat on the bed, far enough away that I couldn't smell her.

"Yes. It. Is."

"This is my room," she said.

I stood and so did Tommie.

We eyed each other.

We were a foot apart. Hands balled into fists. Both of us.

"And Justin is my boyfriend," Tommie said. She jabbed at my chest, not quite touching me.

"Who?"

"Justin."

That guy from the party? I'd seen him today. Had we even spoken?

"What do I care about that?" For some reason I felt dizzy. Pukish.

Worried.

"You," Tommie said, and she took a step closer to me. I moved back toward the door. Why had I closed it? "You are ruining my life. Taking it over. And I"—she took another step. I backed up again—"am sick of it."

I swallowed three times before I could find my voice, which was buried somewhere right near the chicken and veggies.

"You need to leave." The words were whispered. Almost not there. Ghosty.

"Why should I?" Tommie said. "*You* should go."

"JimDaddy," I said, "gave me this room when me and Momma moved in here."

Tommie turned, twirling, arms raised like a ballerina, and floated to the window.

"He won't speak to me," Tommie said after a long minute where I considered on running down the hall to Baby Lucy's room and asking Momma to get a stick or a broom or something, anything, to get this girl out of my room.

But her words slowed me.

"What do you mean?" I asked.

"My daddy," Tommie said. "He stopped talking to me about three years ago."

Icy water feelings dripped all over me.

JimDaddy didn't have a child.

Did he?

I couldn't breathe.

This was not good.

The words arranged themselves in my head in capital print like something from a novel. I knew what had happened.

A TERRIBLE DIVORCE.

Or

HE WAS AN ADULTERER.

Did Momma know?

Aunt Odie's newest creation knocked on my tonsils.

Somehow, JimDaddy the Builder had gotten rid of his wife *and* his daughter and who knew who else. Perhaps he was

A MURDERER.

My blood got all cloggy.

"I better go," Tommie said.

Relief filled me and I caught my breath.

She left the room, the house, without making a sound.

40

What was going on?

41

I mean it.
    What?

42

You know when something goes down the wrong pipe and you nearly choke to death? You can't catch your breath and you feel like you'll die if you don't get air and your eyes stream tears?

That's how I felt.

Only without the choking and the tears part. It was *still* hard to breathe.

Who was this Tommie?

Where did she live (close!) that she could be here so often?

Why wouldn't JimDaddy have anything to do with his girl—almost my age, by the way—from his first marriage?

Better yet, why hadn't he told Momma?

I slowed. Numbed.

Or. Had. He?

I stood. Took one hundred years to make it to the door. Another hundred years to twist the knob and get down the hall to Baby Lucy's room, where Momma was putting my sister down to rest.

"Momma?" I said, when I stood in that doorway. My voice was cotton.

It was getting close to dinner. Now the window was a mirror. I walked across the room and pulled down the shade. Shivered.

Was Tommie back to her home yet? How did she get here? Walk? Ride a bike? Hitchhike?

Momma looked at me, her long hair cascading down her back like a wild waterfall. Baby Lucy, lying in her bed, showed me her tooth.

"What is it, Evie?" Momma finished the diapering. Snapped Lucy's sleeper. Lifted her and kissed her on the face.

Lucy rested her head a moment on my mother's shoulder. Jabbered at me, then yawned.

"Momma." My voice fought to be heard. "JimDaddy was married before. Wasn't he?"

Momma stiffened. Only her eyes moved, looking at me and then away. At me again and away.

It was true!

Adulterer? Murderer? Certainly a divorcer.

My room had been someone else's, and that someone was Tommie.

I whispered, "Why didn't y'all tell me?"

Momma thawed. Patted at Baby Lucy, who cooed like she was answering the question, if I could understand baby talk.

"Listen," Momma said. She raised one hand.

Why, she was trying to come up with something! Are you kidding me? I wasn't sure if I should be mad or furious at her.

"Listen."

"I am."

In the corner of the room, the rocker moved all slow, with a *creak creak creak*.

My heart leaped. Thank goodness for ribs and skin and such. Otherwise I might be heartless at that moment. All three of us stared at the rocker.

"It does that sometimes," Momma said, her voice a murmur.

And I answered, "Oh."

Baby Lucy spoke to the chair. Pumped her little fists.

I swallowed a few times.

Could it be that *she* had the Gift fourteen-plus years early? Was that allowed with us Messengers?

"What's going on, Momma?"

"How should I know? It just happens."

The chair still moved.

"I mean . . ." Should I sit in it? Stop the rocking? A part of me wanted to run. But Momma didn't seem afraid. "I mean about JimDaddy."

"Oh." She shrugged.

"Did he tell you he was married before? Did . . . did you know?"

Momma nodded. Swallowed. Said, "We should wait till JimDaddy gets home to talk about all this."

"I need to know now."

The rocker eased to a stop.

Momma pushed past me and headed to the front room, carrying Baby Lucy.

"You need to tell me. What about his wife? What about his daughter?"

Momma slowed her step as she went down the hall, then sped up again.

"What aren't you telling me?"

But Momma wasn't saying nothing except wait until Jim-Daddy came home.

43

Jeez!

44

I let myself out of the house, slamming the door shut behind me.

Out over the ocean, clouds billowed, growing tall and dark in the late afternoon sky. Looked the way I felt, those clouds did. Lightning illuminated the east.

A voice came from the end of the porch. "Hey, Evie."

I let out a little scream. "What are you doing here, Buddy?" Yellow hibiscus flowers on the bushes behind him bobbed in the breeze.

He sat on the porch swing, his long legs looking grasshopper-like when he tucked them under the swing. The chains cried out. *Wah. Wah. Wah.*

"Just came to see you," he said. He patted the swing. "Come sit over here."

"What is it about people in this neighborhood? Popping out of here and there. Always surprising me." I stayed by the door, the AC swirling outside. "I got homework."

"The first day?"

"Yes." Almost true. I had self-inflicted homework so I

didn't get behind in any of my classes. Plus, there was the homework of picking out what to wear tomorrow.

Buddy smiled that cute smile of his.

"I saved you a place," he said.

Tell me who can sit next to a good-looking boy with gorgeous cheekbones and squinty eyes when she's just found out her momma had married a man who had been married before? A man who was one of three things, none of them that becoming.

Sure, Momma *had* been married before herself. But *my* daddy died when I just learning to walk. Stroke. No one had any idea it was coming.

JimDaddy was a man worse than that super-old actor Alex Baldman in that show *Child Actors and Their Parents*. My stepfather—who had mentioned maybe adopting me—wouldn't even speak to his own flesh-and-blood daughter, Tommie. Why not? His. Own. Flesh. And. Blood. How could this be possible?

We Messengers talk till you wish we'd shut up.

JimDaddy, it seemed, cut off his loved ones. Right at the knees. But didn't get the back door fixed so they couldn't sneak in our house.

So who could sit next to a pretty boy when all this was racing through her brain? I could.

I stomped across the front porch, past the concrete planters filled with petunias that Momma had planted at the beginning of summer, running my fingertips along the porch railing. Then I stood in front of Buddy, my arms folded across my chest.

He patted the wooden slats next to him.

Darn that squinty-eyed smile!

"Right here," he whispered, then opened his hands to me.

I took his hands in my own.

I was a backstabber to women all over the world.

I sat next to Buddy, not even waiting for him to tighten his arm around me, just resting my head against his chest and closing my eyes to the trouble I was sure would come that evening.

45

Maybe Momma was with JimDaddy because sitting next to him made her feel safe.

Maybe she was with him because watching a storm come in from the ocean was comfortable, even with lightning that looked to split Florida in half.

Maybe she was with him because she'd sat on this very porch swing, his arm around her, and had never spoken a word and it had felt perfect.

46

Love.

47

Yes. Love.

48

The storm broke while we were on the front porch, swinging and not talking. Rain poured from the sky like it was the star of a movie, the whole yard appearing too green.

JimDaddy pulled into the drive, lights slicing across the yard. Baby frogs leaped every which way, like they had fallen from the clouds.

"That's my cue," Buddy said. He squeezed me up close. "I'm coming back tonight," he said.

"I should hope so."

He slipped away.

I stood, walked across the front porch, and waited for my stepfather. The porch light sensors went off and it was as though I was center stage, spots shining on me only.

JimDaddy waved and when he eased past, there was a haunted look on his face like he didn't know what was coming— because he didn't. Then he drove into the three-car garage.

49

Love?

50

I came inside, slamming the front door for good measure. I was getting good at this slamming thing. And here it was my first day perfecting the talent.

"Hey, girl," JimDaddy said, coming in through the garage at the same moment.

He moved into the living room and grabbed up Baby Lucy, who was now on her play blanket (short nap?), kicking her feet at the chandelier. He hugged her. Pressed his face to hers. Closed his eyes then kissed her cheek.

"Dadadada," she said. Baby Lucy pulled at JimDaddy's mustache.

"Baby girl, baby girl," JimDaddy said, all soft.

Baby Lucy slapped his face in a patty-cake sorta way.

"Miss me?" he asked.

Momma came in from the kitchen then and watched Baby Lucy give her daddy wet kisses. Momma, who had looked worried and stiff as beaten egg whites, seemed to melt observing the two of them. But she didn't speak. I'm not sure JimDaddy even knew she was behind him.

"Sir," I said, feeling awkward.

JimDaddy laughed. "Sir?" he said. He went to his recliner then, sat, and kicked off his work shoes. He settled back, his face smoothing out like worries slipped away, Baby Lucy sitting on his chest. Closed his eyes. "Since when do you call me sir?"

"Ummm," I said. *Get mad,* I thought. *Get mad and chew him out about Tommie.* But seeing him on the chair with my sister, I couldn't rustle up a smidgen of displeasure. I was grateful he held my sister in that loving way. Grateful we were all together. Even if he'd left his other family behind, or killed people. Well. Maybe not that.

I was a traitor.

A traitor for happiness I had helped to steal from one family—without meaning to.

His daughter.

Like Lucy.

Like *me.*

"Something smells good," JimDaddy said. He seemed to have no energy. In fact, he might have gone to sleep right there.

Momma drifted to his side like a spirit. "You feeling better, Jimmy? Ready to eat?"

Better? Was he . . . panic came up in my heart area . . . was he sick?

Could he have a stroke?

Could he . . . ?

JimDaddy's eyes popped open. He didn't smile but looked at Momma like he had lost her for a moment and just discovered her whereabouts. He reached for her hand, and Momma took his. JimDaddy kissed Momma's knuckles.

I cleared my throat and my stepfather stood, cradling Baby Lucy in one arm. The curtains shifted as the air-conditioning clicked on, like someone walked behind the sheers.

Fish was frying. Corn bread baking. I bet Momma had run down the street to Aunt Odie's place, where she'd been experimenting with a batter "good for chicken or fish." I mean before her newest, newest idea.

"What's going on?" JimDaddy said. He looked too tired for words. Come to think of it, he was looking pretty worn at my birthday party and he stayed awake long past his usual bedtime. Dark circles ringed his eyes.

Momma hurried into the kitchen, gesturing small so only I would see. I gave her the stink eye. She ignored me. I followed, flapping my hands in a *we have to talk* way.

She hoofed it to the stove, pulled catfish from the oil to drain. Said over her shoulder, "Set the table, please?" Her words were rigid. A warning.

And why was that? I hadn't even had a chance to do something wrong. Yet. How was getting the truth a wrong anyway?

"Momma . . ."

"We'll talk while we eat," Momma whispered. She peeked through the kitchen door and nodded at JimDaddy, and Baby Lucy. She looked worried. Momma, not Baby Lucy. Well, Momma should be.

"Wash up?" she asked, like this time might be different from all the other meals I had ever eaten with her.

JimDaddy was over to Momma in three strides, his tie gone, his shirt unbuttoned at the collar. He kissed her full on the mouth, Baby Lucy swinging like a bag of groceries, clutching at the sleeve of his dress shirt.

"Food's gonna burn," I said. But who ever hears the sane one in a family? The dog, maybe. And we don't have a dog.

"I'm sorry," he said, resting his forehead against hers. "I'm trying."

He kissed Momma again.

"I'm trying real hard." His voice got stuck on the last word.

I had to look away.

My mother was laying lips on the man who'd left at least one child and at least one wife on the side of the road. Practically.

"You mind taking her, Evie?" JimDaddy said. "I'm gonna change my clothes."

I kept my head down and reached for the baby as he walked from the room.

Momma smiled like that was the best kiss ever, and I

thought I should run away with Baby Lucy now, taking me with her, while we had a chance, before we were kicked out of our bedrooms and left to sneak into the house the back way.

"Maybe it's getting better," Momma said to no one.

"Dadadadada," Baby Lucy said. I rested my cheek on her head.

"You," Momma said, pointing at me with a greasy spatula, "you better be nice. You don't know this story."

"How can I know anything?" I said. "Y'all haven't said a word to me."

"Just remember I can still give you a pot with five handles."

I almost laughed. "You gonna spank me?"

"No Southern child is too old for a pop on the bottom. Especially if she isn't respecting her elders."

"Whatever," I said with a sigh.

"Wawawawa," said Baby Lucy.

Momma planted her hands on her waist, that spatula dripping oil in blotches on the dark wood floor.

When JimDaddy was back, changed into an old paint-spattered Florida Gators T-shirt, we settled around the table, Lucy perched on Momma's lap so she could eat straight off the plate.

"Grace," Momma said.

"Bless the Messengers and the Fletchers," JimDaddy said. "And this food."

Then we set to eating. Dipping fish in vinegar, slathering

butter on the corn bread, and eating coleslaw that was just-the-right sweet. Momma acted like nothing had happened at all. Just said out of the side of her mouth, "Honey, we got to have a family meeting soon as we finish here."

Waiting, waiting, and more waiting.

After two plates of food, JimDaddy leaned back in his chair. Across the room from us the refrigerator hummed, then clicked off. The room fell silent. Even Baby Lucy didn't say a word. She looked at me and Momma and JimDaddy like she was expecting something too.

"What is it we need to chat about?" JimDaddy said.

Momma dabbed at her lips.

I saw her swallow.

A knot grew in my throat. I chewed hard. Swallowed the bite almost whole.

"She knows," she said.

"She knows what?" JimDaddy said. There was a long stretch of silence and then, "Oh."

JimDaddy looked at his plate.

I stared at the top of his head, where his hair was so blond and thick I wondered if I'd ever find a gray hair.

"Oh," he said again.

"Oh," Lucy said. Her mouth made a perfect oval, like she tasted the word.

So it was true. Something was true.

"How could you?" I asked. The words trembled from me.

For a brief moment I saw Tommie, sitting on my bed, looking at me like she might cry.

"Excuse me?" JimDaddy said. The words were breathy, hollow.

"How could you leave her out there like that?"

"Leave her?" JimDaddy looked like I'd hit him a good one. His face went dark as a storm. He was furious. "Who told you that?" he asked. "Who would say such a thing?"

Your daughter, I wanted to say, but I didn't answer. I could be angry too.

Momma reached for my arm, but I moved away.

JimDaddy straightened in his chair. Moved around like he was getting ready for a meeting with zoning officials. Not that I have ever seen him talking about breaking ground or anything. But maybe he does it this way, with a shift-shift-shifty move.

He glanced at Momma.

Baby Lucy stayed quiet. The whole house stayed quiet. The three of us stared each other around the table, like we played tag with our eyes only.

"Tell her," Momma whispered, and her breath seemed to make the candles flicker till two went out. The third gasped and kept burning.

Fried fish swam in my stomach.

"Tell me," I whispered, and the last candle went out.

JimDaddy grabbed at Baby Lucy, who crawled over the

table from Momma and into his arms. When he spoke, he sounded ready to cry. "Now, Evie. You have to know your momma and me, we decided some things were better left unsaid." He cleared his throat. "Until you asked about them."

Momma nodded.

Fish tried to swim up my gullet, but I swallowed them down.

"Like you were married before?" My voice sounded hot even to my own ears. I did not look at my mother. A sound came from the back door. Like the doorknob jiggled. Did Tommie try to get inside?

"Yes, like that."

"But," Momma said, "there's more to the story."

"Much more," JimDaddy said.

"Oh," said Baby Lucy.

"So tell me," I said, though I was sure I might scram as soon as the details were revealed.

JimDaddy pressed his nose into Lucy's neck. Three tears leaked from his eye. Yes, just one eye. And three tears. Like one for each of us. He looked straight at me. "Here's what happened, Evie."

51

"I've known your momma my whole life."

"Yes," Momma said.

The doorknob jiggled again. Outside the wind grew from nothing at all to a gust that made the trees bow. Lightning marked up the sky, and the streetlights flickered on.

"I always had a secret crush on her."

Momma smiled.

"But we went our separate ways and your momma married your daddy and I . . ." JimDaddy took a breath. "I married Cindy Hastings."

I waited. Silent. No one said anything for so long I got antsy. I said, "And . . ."

JimDaddy kissed Lucy, who clutched a bit of fish, like she was nervous too.

"We were danged happy, me and Cindy. I saw your momma now and again. Knew when you were born, 'cause we had us a daughter a year before. We named her Tommie."

Ice water splashed over my head. The doorknob stopped

its jiggling. I slapped my hands on the table. "I knew it," I said.

JimDaddy took another deep breath. "The two of them were killed three years ago. In a car accident."

"You remember the accident, don't you, Evie?" Momma said. "I told you."

"What do you mean killed?" I asked. I couldn't feel my lips.

"My first wife and daughter are dead," JimDaddy said.

Something sort of stirred in my brain. Something that felt like a million years ago.

"They were the light of my eye. My wife and I only had the one child. And then they went together." His voice cracked.

Now it sounded like the whole of outside became lightning and thunder and birds calling and frogs croaking and mosquitoes buzzing and snakes slithering and cracking voices and my heart? My heart might have stopped.

Now my head filled up with too much noise. Now I glanced at the doorknob and saw it turn.

Momma spoke then, and I could hear only parts of what she had to say. Words like, "We didn't want you to know yet." And "New furniture for your room that used to be Tommie's." And "She would be sixteen."

I stood so fast the dining room chair toppled to the floor. My glass of Coke spilled across the table and Baby Lucy said, "Uh-oh."

My head swam. I was going to faint. Faint.

Dead?

Tommie?

No!

No!

I wouldn't have it!

I wouldn't!

52

Gift or no, I was done!

53

I stormed down the street in the rain and straight into Aunt
Odie's house without even knocking. The door popped against
the entryway hall, and I didn't even bother to close it.

Why should I?

She . . .

She . . .

"Aunt Odie?"

TV noise came from the family room.

I hurried down the hall and past the kitchen.

Aunt Odie looked up at me from a huge flat-screen, where
she watched a recording of *Judge Judy*. If there is anything I
can say about my aunt, and there is a whole lot, it's that she is
a *Judge Judy* fan. She never watches cooking shows. "Don't
want to be influenced," she's said. "I got a direct line to a
spiritual world. No need to mess with the living on this one."

But *Judge Judy*? Aunt Odie loves a woman with spine.
Her words. Not mine.

"Aunt Odie!"

"Hey, sugar," Aunt Odie said. She glanced at me, then came to attention in her chair.

"What? What?" she said.

"Dead people!" I said. "I see dead people!"

Aunt Odie picked up the remote and clicked the TV to pause. Right as Judge Judy was saying, "Young lady, you can't just appear and disappear in people's lives and not expect consequences of some sort."

"And you knew it!"

Judge Judy's mouth was stuck open, freeze-frame.

"I thought someone had died, the way you looked around the eyes."

I stomped up to her. To my aunt. Not Judge Judy. "Someone *has* died. Lots have. Did you hear me? I. See. Dead. People." My hands were fists now.

Aunt Odie settled. "What are you saying?"

"You. Knew." The words were full of accusation.

The whole house smelled of lemons. What had she been cooking? I didn't care. I mean, I'd care later. After this war was over. After we'd talked.

"What do you mean?" she asked.

"What do you mean, what do I mean?"

Aunt Odie fanned at herself with a *Family Circle* magazine. "So it happened."

I nodded. In a violent sorta way.

"Oh no." Aunt Odie stood, walked around a moment, then

moved to the leather sectional. She sat on the sofa, still fanning, then let out a breath. "I wondered when. I wondered when. At first I thought there was a hole in the system. Thought something strange had happened."

"Are you kidding? Something strange *has* happened." My heart pounded so I could see my shirt moving.

Where was Tommie right now? Where? Looking in a window? Sitting on a toilet? Jingling a doorknob somewhere? Chills slipped over me like a bodysuit.

My aunt patted the sofa next to her, shaking her head as though she was the one sad and sorrowful. "You figured it out."

I didn't move. Felt my face go squishy.

"Hand me a cigarette, will you, honey? My nerves are undone."

But I didn't. I stood there with my hands on my hips. I was furious. Betrayed. I was so angry I could . . . Well, not die. I'd never say *that* again.

"You are a little bent out of shape, now, aren't ya?" Aunt Odie blinked several times like she had pepper in her eyes. "I see that."

I jabbed a finger at Aunt Odie. *My* eyes filled with tears. "Paulie told you, didn't he? The other day, he said . . ." I couldn't keep talking.

She nodded. "He said you have a rare gift."

I gawked at her. I mean really gawked. Like it says in books.

"And you didn't say anything about it. Nothing! Why?"

Aunt Odie studied her fingernails, then looked up at me. "Because nothing had happened. And I didn't want to get you all worked up over something that might prove false. Come on, cinnamon bear. Sit down."

I refused to sit. I stood there, towering over Aunt Odie, who looked up at me with a guilty expression on her face.

"Honey," she said at long last. "I wasn't sure Paulie was right. I mean, I get recipes from dreams. My aunt before me could read minds. You should have heard what she said President Roosevelt was thinking. Her aunt before her could grow anything, *anything*, and then heal people with her herbs. And you know what your momma and aunts can do."

I didn't move.

Aunt Odie shook her head. "I didn't know you were going to get the dead-people card. Few are trusted with that."

"Cards or not," I said, "this shouldn't be happening."

"Now wait," Aunt Odie said.

"It isn't fair."

My aunt put on her *nothing in life is fair* look, but to my surprise, she didn't say that. Instead she stood, pulled me close, and hugged me. Tight. A little too tight. She whispered into my hair. "Some's more special than others. Prophets aren't looking for the calling."

"I'm not a prophet," I said into her shoulder. I wanted to

pull away, but hugging my aunt was too comfortable. "And what's Momma gonna say? I have a strong feeling she has an aversion to ghosts."

Aunt Odie patted my back. "She knows. I told her what Paulie said."

"Oh." I pushed back from Aunt Odie. "I've been seeing one ghost all along and didn't even know it. For all I know, you're dead."

She put both hands on my shoulders. "Could be, but I'm not. I've a feeling we better make us another trip to Cassadaga."

Judge Judy was frozen mid-move—pointing at someone, mouth wide, eyes serious. From the kitchen I heard the timer ding. "Are you cooking something?"

"I'm always cooking something. Listen. I'll call Paulie. Let him know you and me are coming out tomorrow morning before school starts. You okay for an early morning trip?"

"Not really," I said.

"And I need you tomorrow. Think you can get rid of this sour mood?" I gave her a look and she hurried on with, "We got to fill a lot of orders." She went in the kitchen and I heard the oven door open, then shut.

I stood quiet, a lemon smell swirling around me. "Why is she here?" I said when Aunt Odie eased back into the room.

"Who?"

"The girl. JimDaddy's first child."

"Good golly," Aunt Odie said. She took a breath deep enough to shift her spleen. "That *is* a sour card, Evie."

"I know. What do I do?"

"You're gonna have to figure that one out."

54

The sun had set when I walked home (and I only went after Momma called me and said I *had* to get on back to do homework). The moon was shadowed by clouds. The streets and sidewalks were wet. Lots of people had turned on their indoor lights. Some left their curtains open. Including at Buddy's place. I stopped on the sidewalk.

A woman played a huge piano.

A dog sat near her.

"That is one big dog," I said to no one. And where was Buddy? I stretched this way and that, looking through the picture window for him.

"Hey, Evie."

This time I kept my yelp under control.

"What are you doing out here, Buddy?" I said. Pleased and surprised all at once. He'd come up close and his arm touched mine. I smiled in the darkness. Turned to look up at him.

Buddy took my hand. "I told you, Evie. I'm coming to kiss you." His voice was low.

I grinned even bigger.

"Good," I said, feeling brave. "I need the distraction."

"I intend to be more than a distraction, Evie Messenger."

Buddy pulled me near.

Bent closer.

His lips found mine.

"Mmm," he said. Buddy's arms went around me. Pulled me so tight I thought to push away. But no. I needed this. This hot guy kissing me. I needed Tommie out of my head. And Aunt Odie and Paulie and school and JimDaddy and dead wives and new wives and children, gone, gone, gone. The whole kit and kaboodle.

"Let's go sit," Buddy said, and led me across my wet front lawn and onto the porch, where a light flicked on when we got near enough for the sensor to know we were there.

"Can't kiss in the light," I said. I was whispering and my lips tingled. No longer numb. Good. "My momma is waiting for me." We sat on the swing that was damp under my bottom.

Tommie. Tommie. In my head. In my room? Waiting for me?

"*I've* been waiting for you longer, Evie," Buddy said. He used both his hands to try and tame my hair that had swelled as soon as I walked out of Aunt Odie's house.

"Have you?"

"Yes, ma'am."

He gave up on my hair (I think) and cupped my face in his hands.

Ran his finger over my lips.

"If we don't move," he said, "that light might go out. We're out of range."

I took his hand in mine. He was so warm. And he smelled like orange rolls. Had his momma made one of Aunt Odie's mixes?

The porch light went out, and just like that Momma opened the door. "Evie," she said.

"I'm here, Momma."

"Who're you with?"

"Buddy from across the way."

Momma hesitated. Light spilled out from the house, and she looked dark as a ghoul. Only ghouls aren't dark. At least not girl ghosts, who aren't really ghouls at all.

"Fifteen minutes," Momma said, and shut the door quick.

The spotlight stayed off.

"That's no time at all," Buddy said.

"Then let's not waste it."

How could I do this?

How could I know how to kiss my across-the-street-neighbor when I had never kissed anyone before? (Not including Tommy Jones, who in first grade said, "Knock knock," and I said, "Who's there?" and he said, "Olive," and I said, "Olive who?" and he said, "Olive you," and kissed me half on the mouth and half on the nose, for which I slapped him a good one, *and* AJ Moorman in sixth grade, who caught me unawares in the lunchroom right when I was ready to throw my empty lunch bag away. He tasted a lot like mustard.)

How did I know what to do with my mouth and tongue and teeth? And lips? Can't forget the lips.

"Evie," Buddy said. He sounded breathless. "I've never kissed anyone like you."

I'm a natural, I wanted to say. Maybe this could be my age fifteen Gift from the other side. Not the ghost thing. But I didn't say anything at all, just kissed Buddy those few minutes, like I might never do it again.

"Who have you kissed, Buddy? Lot of girls?" *He* seemed like a professional.

"I've had plenty of girlfriends," he said. He rested his forehead on mine. "But none kissed me like that."

Was that a line? I didn't even care.

"Anyone from school?"

Why was I asking? It's not like we were going out. Were we? Were we? But that kissing mouth of mine made me ask.

He was so nice to look at.

Was it because it was dark out?

Because the whole place smelled of ocean?

"I've only had one serious girlfriend," he said. Buddy pulled away from me.

I rested in his arms.

"We were young. And knew it."

He swallowed. Twice. I heard him.

"She was killed . . ."

Wait!

". . . killed . . ."

No!

". . . in a car accident a few years back."

Don't say it!

"Justin?" My voice came out a whisper. "Are you Justin?"

"She lived right here in this house. Off and on."

Are. You. Kidding. Me?

"Her name was . . ."

"Tommie," we said together.

55

"You have *got* to stop sneaking up on me," I said before I even turned on my light. I knew Tommie would be in my room when I slammed the door behind me, Buddy—or should I call him *Justin*—still sitting on the swing saying, "What? I don't know what I did," and me saying, "Time's up. I gotta go in now."

Tommie seemed suspended in the air in the corner of the room.

"I am not sneaking. This is *my* room."

I threw my clothes off and into a pile next to the rocker, then crawled into the bed in just my panties. I didn't even brush my teeth. Or put on a shirt. So there!

Or wash my face, and Buddy's smell was all over my skin. Was that cologne? My heart flipped around. I settled the sheet over my body. Thank goodness the AC was on. One thing about kissing is it raises one's internal temperature. And one thing about JimDaddy is he is not a tightwad contractor. Nope. He just withholds important information about a star witness.

I flopped onto my side, away from where Tommie glowed in the corner.

"Gotta sleep," I said.

When she spoke, she was right near my ear. He voice was sad as I expected a dead girl's voice to be. Now that I knew she was dead, I mean. Really dead.

"I saw you with him."

Could she strangle me, right here in bed, like in the movies?

Would she?

I touched my throat.

Tommie sniffed.

"Justin was my first and only boyfriend," she said, and her words were brokenhearted.

Like that I remembered walking in on Momma when I was about six years old, and she was crying like she might never stop because my real daddy was gone and I wouldn't ever remember him.

Did the dead feel as heartbroken as the leftover living? How fair was that?

"We were going to get married."

Married? She'd only been twelve or thirteen. . . .

"*He* didn't know. I'd made those secret plans in my

heart. Even found a wedding dress and saved it online."

I looked at nothing in the dark.

"You were kissing him, Evie."

"Listen, Tommie," I said, and sat up, keeping the sheet up around my neck.

But she was gone.

56

The next morning, me, Momma, and Baby Lucy got up early so we could talk and have breakfast together as a family. *With* JimDaddy. He told me everything, and I listened, squeezing Baby Lucy tight like a boa constrictor. Nah, not really. But she did look at me, brows furrowed, when I gave her a little more hugging than necessary.

"Sorry, Baby," I said, my lips in her curls.

Momma wiped down the kitchen counters. They gleamed. The sink sparkled. I could tell she stayed on the edge of things so she could hear what we had to say to each other.

I glanced at the doorknob. Shivered.

"You listening?" Momma asked.

"Yes, ma'am."

I was listening all right.

Tommie was nowhere to be seen. Did she watch us? See us all the time? Even in the bathroom?

Yuck.

This is what JimDaddy said:

Him and his wife were separated for more than two years. (Separated before their divorce? More news to me.)

He got the house (this house, with the jiggly doorknob) because his ex moved, with Tommie, to Daytona.

He'd let Tommie redecorate her room, and they spent every other weekend together *and* three days every other week (the best parts of his life), and then Tommie and her mother were killed in a car accident after visiting him.

"Me," JimDaddy said. "It was raining and I insisted my ex bring Tommie here after they all went to the show. It was my time. My time to see my baby. I didn't care but that I got it. No matter the weather."

His voice rose. "You know how it rains in the summer."

His eyes filled with tears that didn't fall.

I nodded.

Momma looked like she had witnessed the wreck with her very own eyes.

JimDaddy said, "Your momma and me, we'd started dating a few months before the accident, Evie."

Momma turned away then. Walked over to the stove. She had stopped stirring the oatmeal, and I could hear the bubbles popping, making a for-sure mess on the stove. Momma gathered her hair with one hand, kept her back to me. Was she crying? About Tommie? For her husband?

"You were together that long before you said anything to

me?" I said. "I mean, I knew you were around but I didn't *know* know."

"It wasn't her fault." JimDaddy's voice dropped to almost nothing. "She told me about you, and I couldn't bring myself to meet you. Not for more than a year. I couldn't."

I nodded. Remembering. Remembering how Momma said to me one day, out of the blue, "If Jim Fletcher doesn't meet you soon, we are done." I'd said, "Who?" "Someone I've been seeing," Momma had said. She'd wept for a week, too, after that announcement.

So what? I hadn't met my gonna-be stepfather. I hadn't cared one way or another if Momma stayed or went.

Except.

Except Momma was broken up about not being with him. I could see that. Those days grief was all over her face. In lines and worry and sadness.

"Whatever," I had said. I was watching an old *Legend of Korra* show when Momma mentioned the ultimatum.

Not two weeks later Momma took me to meet JimDaddy, and he stared at me a good long time, not saying a word, just adjusting his tie ('cause we were at his office with the indoor palm trees), and then he'd scooped me up and held me tight for a long time. I hadn't dared to move.

It's uncomfortable when a strange man grabs onto you like that.

"She looks like you," JimDaddy had said. They were married not long after.

Now I stood, Baby Lucy on my hip.

When JimDaddy talked, I could hear the anguish. Could see it sweating off him. Could smell it on his breath. It was too much.

"I still miss her," he whispered. "Them."

And he cried.

My heart twisted.

"I gotta get, Momma. Me and Aunt Odie are headed back to Cassadaga."

I handed Baby Lucy to my stepfather, then walked out of the door and down the street to my aunt's house, trying to breathe all the fresh Florida air I could get to keep the sadness away.

57

That whole thing.

That whole thing was awful.

Seeing JimDaddy, crying like that.

Let me forget, I thought, and ran the rest of the way to Aunt Odie's.

58

Too many people to avoid now.

JimDaddy.

Buddy.

And worst of all, Tommie.

Paulie better have something to tell me.

Yes, he better.

59

Paulie waited on the front porch. Aunt Odie (who was sworn off girdles, even around Paulie) and him didn't gaze at each other or look at each other or giggle.

"Girl," he said. "Odie."

He was so tall, Paulie almost had to duck to get back into his house/place of business.

There were the walls, purple as a bruise. And there was that sign, blue-eyed, trembling out the invitation for someone to come on in. And here we were. My knees felt weak as cake batter.

This morning the sky was full of promises. No rain at all. Not that I could see. Fog settled over the grass, swirling like something moved through it. Paulie gestured for us like he had things to do, and we went into the darkened home.

"What you got for us, Paulie?" Aunt Odie said.

Both of them were down to business. No time to waste. Give me what you got.

"Sit," he said. "Same places as before. Can't disturb structure."

I sat. They did too.

Paulie didn't reach for my hand this time. He cleared his throat, pulled a plate of shortbread cookies out of the darkness, then two cups of coffee and a glass of milk.

The coffee overpowered the smell of sweet butter. My stomach buckled. What was Tommie doing now? Or Buddy? I hadn't spoken to *him* in hours. Hadn't responded to calls, hadn't responded to his texts. Nothing.

"You sure we have time for this?" Aunt Odie said, then sipped at the coffee before Paulie could answer.

"Lookit," I said. Something crawled up the back of my throat. I gulped. Hard. "I gotta go to school. We *don't* have time to linger."

"My recipe," Aunt Odie said. She popped a cookie in her mouth. "Good job, Paulie."

"Thank you."

"I said," I said.

"We heard you." Aunt Odie wasn't mad. Just doing what she does second best. Eating. First best, cooking. First-first best, loving nieces.

"The girl's right," Paulie said. He sipped at *his* coffee too, then leaned back in his chair.

"You won't be late," Aunt Odie said. "I'll run you right up to the door."

That I could believe. Aunt Odie driving across the front

lawn of the high school, under the flag, and down the sidewalk to my classroom.

Darkness settled around us. When I glanced toward the window, I could see the day, but no light seemed to pass the glass.

"It's like this, Evie," Paulie said. "We all got Gifts, right? Everyone, near about in your family, they are aware of what they can do."

"That's right," Aunt Odie said. "Go ahead and drink some, eat a cookie." She handed me three.

Out of nervousness, I chugged at the milk that was cold as a Popsicle. Brain freeze. Brain freeze!

Paulie's voice didn't have a lot of ups and downs to it. He droned on, Aunt Odie interrupting. My head ached. My eyes were raw.

"Some people reach in and pull at the sensitive areas."

"Now Paulie," Aunt Odie said.

"Get your mind out of the gutter," Paulie said, and they both laughed.

The pain was gone and I could see now.

"There're people like me who sense things, like the future. Or worries of the living and dead. Helping in ways I can."

Could see the shape of the room.

"There are people like your aunt, who get messages from the dead. Or your momma, who has inherited her abilities."

Could see the furniture. The lamps. The woven rugs on the floor.

"Then some, they can taste what a spirit wants you to know. Others smell direction. Still others hear voices."

Could see the family waiting on the sofa. The dad, who checked his watch. The mom, who held a baby on her lap. A little girl, who stood next to her father, hand on his knee.

"Remember Horton Hendley?" Aunt Odie said. "She lets spirits take over her body to communicate to loved ones." Aunt Odie ate another cookie. "Remember that, Paulie?" She turned to me. "Horton resides in Pensacola."

Okay.

He nodded, smiling, his teeth like Chiclets. "Special gift, for sure."

"Sure is a pretty thing," Aunt Odie said. "She sure is."

And the man waiting in a wingback chair, hat in hands.

And the crowd at the windows.

That's why the sun wouldn't come in. Too many people.

Wait.

Wait, wait, wait.

I sipped at the milk again, hand trembling, and the door bulged with more waiting people, pushing, trying, silent. And there was Tommie.

"Tommie?" She was gone at her name.

"Excuse me?" Paulie said, and Aunt Odie put her hand on my arm, a hand as hot as an iron.

"And you, Evie, you have a little bit of it all—with the gifts and privileges of seeing the dead. Communicating. Socializing. Healing."

The dead.

All around us.

Right now.

"Uh."

"Now drink your milk." Aunt Odie pat-patted me. "We gotta git."

People pressed in around the table. They all looked so . . . worried. So helpless. No one said anything.

"Now listen," Paulie said, pushing back his chair. He took a hat from the man standing close behind him and put it on his own head. "You concentrate. Rein in the Gift. Control it. Don't let it control you."

"That hat," I said, pointing. My words were like the fog.

Paulie ran his hands around the brim. "My favorite," he said. And then, "Focus, Evie. You can do it."

60

"Focus, Evie."

I should be scared.

Terrified.

A wall had come down. A curtain had been opened.

I could see them all here. Milling about. Crowding inside.

But I wasn't afraid. I shifted. Closed my eyes.

They didn't seem to want anything from me. Of course not. They waited to see Paulie.

I peered at them again. There were no severed limbs. No blood. No guts.

Just people, all shapes and sizes and ages and colors, who moved without effort, who had varying degrees of light coming from their skin.

"They're worried," I said.

"You need to focus, Evie."

No, I wanted to say, you *focus, Paulie. This house of yours is full of spirits waiting for . . . for what?*

I didn't tell Paulie. No way. He might faint knowing what

I saw in his front room and out on the porch and in the line waiting to come into this place. I guess I would have said, *At least they're acting all mannerly. No one's pushing and shoving.*

As me and Aunt Odie got in the Cadillac to drive off, another car pulled in. A true flesh-and-blood car. A man in a suit climbed out of the Kia, and from the line of ghosts that made its way around the house (close enough to touch the building) stepped a woman in a short skirt and jacket. Her hair was done up nice. She drifted over to him, her body trembling a little like Jell-O does if you hit into the table. Her glow grew as they neared each other.

"Go on in," Aunt Odie said when the man hesitated on the first step. The dead pushed near. The woman tried to take the man's hand. "Paulie's the best. You looking to find your future?"

"No, I lost my sister," he said. His face was like a broken dish.

The woman gazed at me. She said, "You tell Warren it's okay," and I could smell roses. "My passing is still new for him. For us." She pressed her hand to her chest. "Tell him things are fine."

I looked at Aunt Odie. She put the car in reverse. A shiver ran right up my spine. It felt like my nerves played in my hair, making knots.

The woman slid to the window and I almost screamed. "Tell him," she said.

Aunt Odie said, "I cannot wait to get me something hot for breakfast. My stomach's growling. You hear it?"

"Yes, ma'am," I said all whispery. Even my eyebrows felt electrified.

"Let's git," Aunt Odie said just as the woman said, "Now, please. If you don't mind. If it's not too much trouble."

The sun broke the horizon, slicing through clouds. The mist burned off the yard and the dew glittered like baubles.

"Wait," I said to Aunt Odie. "Stop."

The car rolled a few feet more as she slowed.

The man knocked on the door now, and I could hear Paulie calling out that we should go, he had an appointment and did we want to scare away business?

"Mister."

He knocked again, and Paulie opened the door wide. "Go on now," he said, waving at us. He wore that hat. Why? To the man he said, "Just family. Come on in, Mr. Bargio. They're leaving."

"Hey. Mister." I tried to holler, but my throat was coated with his sorrow and I couldn't say it louder than the sound a mouse makes on a lamp shade.

But he heard me. Mr. Bargio turned. His face was drawn. Sad. His eyes broke my heart.

"She said . . ." I gulped air like a fish pulled out of the water. "Your sister said, 'It's okay.'"

Mr. Bargio hesitated.

All of the dead looked at me. All of them.

"Excuse me?"

"It's okay," I said. "She said it's okay. She's fine. And then to the others, "I can't help you. I gotta get to school."

"You saw her?" Mr. Bargio asked.

I nodded.

"Is there anything else?"

I shook my head. "No. Not that she said to me."

Paulie, Mr. Bargio, and the dead stared at me.

Aunt Odie mighta swallowed her tongue.

"Let's git," I said.

61

"You gonna tell me what just happened?" Aunt Odie rested one hand on the steering wheel. With the other she patted at my wrist, where I'd tied a friendship bracelet the first day of summer. I saw now the string was grubby. Me and Pearl would have to make new ones. This had flour crusted on it.

"No," I said, and kept my eyes on the road for more of the dead. They gathered, I saw, at all the shops here in Cassadaga. They wandered close to the buildings, like they were looking for a place to shop. Walked up steps. Stood on covered porches. Marched down the sides of the road. Touched the houses.

"Sure you can't talk about it?"

The sun blinded me.

"I'm sure."

62

It was too sacred to talk about.

63

I didn't know anything about this Gift, except that.

The dead being here was sacred.

64

At first I thought they would be everywhere, like in that movie from a million years ago about the kid who sees the dead.

But they weren't. The throngs thinned out as soon as we left Cassadaga. There was a straggler or two headed into town.

But the farther from Cassadaga we drove, the fewer there were.

Did they need to communicate with the living? Did they need Paulie, and all the others, who read palms and tea leaves and tarot cards?

And there. There they were in the graveyard, right there at the edge of that old churchyard.

Fine! That made sense! But why was Tommie at my place?

She needed to take a trip west to Cassadaga. I'd tell her so today.

65

But Tommie *had* been there. If only for an instant. I'd seen her right there at Paulie's.

66

Aunt Odie dropped me off at school with a, "I'll make sure to bring you some lunch, 'kay, punkin?"

I gave her a wave over my head, surging into the school with the crowd. I didn't even look back. I had work to do. Avoiding-Buddy-slash-Justin-slash-my-first-almost-real-boyfriend-slash-why-hadn't-he-told-me-about-Tommie-sooner?

More in depth? Like, everything?

Kids pushed against me, laughing, hollering. I heard someone clear a loogie out of his throat and spit. Several girls squealed, "Ew!"

I couldn't bother with any of that. I rushed to my locker.

Buddy stood there, looking sweeter than cream and prettier than Aunt Odie's best cake. He wore a T-shirt the color of lake water, and even from across the hall I could see his eyes.

"Evie," he said when he saw me, and his expression lit up like the sun this morning burning off the dew.

My heart slammed in my chest. I turned, fast, and went empty-armed toward class.

I ran into three people trying to get away from Buddy. One guy nearly knocked me down but caught me around the waist as I went flying and pulled me onto my feet.

"Evie!"

Over the intercom, the vice principal said something about teachers and a three fifteen meeting. A group of cheerleaders blocked the hall a ways down. They were doing a cheer. In the hall of all places. Why? Lots of people had gathered to watch them. Why again?

I rushed through the line at, "Gimme a *D*!"

"Buddy," someone said. A girl.

I didn't look back. Not all the way, I mean. Buddy ran past one cheerleader, who had broken out of formation and now followed him.

"Not now, Kelly," he yelled. And, "Evie, why are you running from me?"

Up ahead was the bathroom. I'd just go there. Wait. Catch my breath. Worry about this morning and Mr. Bargio's sister and all those people looking so sad. Worry about Tommie and Momma and JimDaddy.

Buddy grabbed my arm. The bell rang. The hall cleared.

Then it was just the two of us.

"Get to class," a teacher called, and shut the door.

"Why are you trying to get away?" Buddy said. I could smell spearmint.

Then he grabbed me and kissed me so hard I thought I'd lose my breath. His hands were warm and the kiss was warm and—not here in the hall, right here at school, where Tommie might be spying.

"Buddy," I said, though he still kissed me. "Buddy." My voice was a whisper.

I pulled away and plowed into the bathroom.

67

I stared at myself in the mirror. My face was flushed from the best kiss I had ever experienced. I gasped for air. Leaned against the sink. Thought to swoon.

Buddy knocked on the door.

"Evie, come on out. Please."

Tommie peeked out of a stall.

"What are you doing in here?"

"What do *you* do in here?" she said. She gave me a disgusted look, and I went to the sink. Would I see her in the mirror? I glanced one-eyed past my image. Yup. There she was. Not a thing like a vampire. Not that I had ever seen a vampire in a mirror. Or anywhere for that matter.

"Ummm," I said. I splashed water on my face.

"Right," she said.

Spirits needed to potty? Okay. After this morning, I'd believe anything. All those ghosts. That kiss. All those ghosts. That . . .

Buddy. "Evie?" *Tap, tap, tap.* "Evie."

Water dripped off my nose.

Tommie tilted her head. "Is that . . ." She paused. Pointed at the door. "Is that Justin?"

My skin seemed too hot. My fingers shook.

Why was I meeting a ghost in a school bathroom after kissing her used-to-be boyfriend in the hall? That seemed . . . wrong. No. Unfair.

And meeting? This was not a scheduled encounter.

"Evie!"

I pushed the door open a crack. "Not now, Buddy. Please!"

He deflated right in front of my eyes. Got shorter. His face went bright red. His shoulders slumped.

I stepped into the hall and threw my arms around his neck. Hugged him so tight I bet he couldn't breathe easy.

"I gotta . . ."

What? Talk to a ghost who's hounding me? And not just any ghost—the ghost who wanted to marry you?

Buddy held me by the shoulders. "You don't have to explain anything to me, Evie," he said. He let me go, tucked his hands in his pockets, and walked away. Maybe even *sauntered* away.

My heart leaped watching him.

I turned back to the bathroom. Unhappy now. I was being followed by the dead. Or whatever you called this. Haunted! That was it. I was being haunted.

So what if that group of the dead at Paulie's had a sacred

feel. This one was downright bugging me. And by the way, she wasn't glowing. Jell-O-y? Yes. Glowing, no.

And anyway, what about all those famous ghosts? Didn't Bloody Mary show up in bathrooms? Or Freddy Krueger?

This I did not want to know. I walked into the restroom, hands out, eyes squinched shut.

"What are you doing?" Tommie asked.

I opened my eyes and glared at her.

She glided over to where I stood. Leaned against the sink. Her hair looked perfect. She wore the same clothes as she always did. But there was that smell. Sour.

"Justin was talking to you," she said. Her eyes, brown and huge—like JimDaddy's—seemed let down. Disappointed. When she spoke again, she whispered. "He doesn't speak to me anymore either."

I wiped my hands on my blue jeans.

"My own momma is gone."

Wiped my forehead with my arm.

"I can't get anyone to talk to me."

She didn't know.

"Only you." Tommie turned to face me.

She didn't know she was dead.

"You are my onliest friend, Evie Messenger."

My heart pounded like a racehorse's hooves.

"I'm scared."

"Me too," I said.

Tell her, my brain said.

No. Never. It wasn't my place.

But it is, my brain said. *This is part of the Gift.*

"No!" I said.

"Excuse me?" Tommie's eyes were too sad to look at.

Do it! Brain said.

Tommie came closer. "What's the matter with you, Evie? Are you losing sight of me too?" Her voice was light as a breath of air.

I took a deep breath. "No. I'm still here. I can see you fine."

She smiled. The full-blown smile I imagined her father missed most of all.

"I'm not sure what I've done that people ignore me." Now she gazed at me in her mirror. Tried to turn on the faucet so she could wash her ghosty hands that looked like real hands.

I ran my palm under the sensor for her.

"Thank you," she said.

I was at the dryer now. My hands wet (drying your hands on your own clothes only works so well). My throat closed up.

The bell rang, blasting. Oh my gosh, I was going to be late to class. I could hear doors being opened in the halls. Could hear people calling for one another, laughing, just a few feet away. Where was Buddy? Three girls burst into the bathroom. I didn't recognize any of them, and they pretended they didn't see me, walking past and into stalls, talking about chemistry being the worst class ever.

Tommie drifted over to where I stood.

"I'm awful lonely."

Not so sure Tommie still spoke to me. Maybe just talking.

My legs shook.

She waved her hands under the hand dryer, but nothing happened.

Did it again.

Again.

Have you ever tried to choke down a brick? I had to open my mouth to breathe.

Tommie and I stood eye to eye. "I can never make this work," she whispered. "*You* turn it on."

"Freak, why are you just standing there?" one girl said. She watched me, hands on her hips. Her friends came out of the stalls.

I glanced at the girls. Then back at Tommie.

"You're dead," I said. And started the dryer with a swish of my hand.

68

"And what is that supposed to mean?" Bathroom Girl said.

I didn't answer. Just watched Tommie melt into the tile floor. Saw a bit of glow follow her, like she was being chased by lightning bugs.

Really? Was the magic word "dead"? Like "please" or "thank you"?

"I said," the girl said, grabbing onto my shoulder and trying to manhandle me around, "are you threatening me?"

I guessed it sounded like I was, if you looked at each little word.

"Don't you take that crap, Leslie," her brunette friend said.

"She *was* threatening you," her other friend said.

Leslie came so close I could smell garlic (this early?) on her breath and Nicki Minaj perfume.

"I wasn't even talking to you," I said. "Get a life."

And I left the building.

69

Not really.

I walked out past Tommie, back from the floor, who made a swipe at my arm and missed.

I will tell you one thing. Seeing ghosts gives you more courage when you're looking in the face of a skinny bully with braces.

Also, Momma and me took a self-defense course a couple of years back.

That helped a lot.

70

Telling a ghost she's dead isn't as easy as you'd think.

They don't *poof!* away. After they dissolve into the floor, they reappear and stay on you. Tail you down the halls. Into your next classes.

Follow you to the door to where someone like Buddy might be standing, waiting, too.

The whole time they're crying.

Saying things like *Prove it! Prove it! Prove I'm dead!*

Trying to make you look at them, see them, pay attention.

Standing on that bridge between the living and the dead is not so easy. 'Cause yes, the dead can see you, but so can the living.

71

After the final bell, Buddy stepped in front of me. Students hurried to the parking lot that was filled with catcalls, horns honking, and engines starting. The sun was so bright, I couldn't see at first. The heat was a blanket. It felt more-than-normal humid out here after the air-conditioned school. Like stepping into a damp rag and using it as a cloak.

"Evie," Buddy said, walking over. He held his hand out. "Evie."

Oh, I wanted to storm past Buddy. And I sort of did. I mean I slowed some. Made it off the sidewalk. Didn't look at him. Tried not to remember that kiss.

Oh, that kiss.

A salty breeze blew past.

The beach.

I would go to the beach.

There was time before I had to work with Aunt Odie and see Momma and Baby Lucy and JimDaddy and do homework.

I'd call Momma and tell her. Use my birthday phone (that

had calls and messages only from Momma and JimDaddy and Aunt Odie on it. And Buddy. Plenty from Buddy. And lots of Pearl. Pearl! I'd almost let my best friend get lost in this weirdo life I was stuck in the middle of). I could figure things out listening to the waves crash on the shore. Hearing the cry of the seagulls. Standing in the surf.

"Evie," Buddy said. "Talk to me. Please. I don't know what I did." He was beside me now. "Again. I keep messing up and I'm not sure what I'm doing. Or what *you're* doing."

I looked up into his eyes.

He didn't know. How could he? But wasn't there a law, somewhere, that said if you had a girlfriend who died, she shouldn't be allowed to haunt your next almost-girlfriend?

If not, there should be.

Not that I was Buddy's almost-girlfriend. Not yet. Would I ever be?

"I'm going to the beach," I said.

Someone flew past in a red Camaro, radio blasting. They beeped and Buddy raised a hand at them.

"I'll take you," he said.

So I let him.

72

Buddy turned the AC on full blast, and we trailed out of the high school parking lot, headed east.

I let out a sigh that seemed to come from the marrow of my bones.

I. Was. So. Tired.

Ghosts, mix-making, and early-hours traipsing all over Florida can do that to you.

I dropped my book bag.

Realized I hadn't seen Tommie since I stepped outside.

Not once.

Why not?

I checked the backseat, looking for her.

"This place is a mess," I said. Maybe ghosts didn't like dirty cars.

"Thank you," Buddy said. He grabbed my hand. Held it in his. His fingers so warm. He cleared his throat.

I looked out the side window. Groups of kids walked on the sidewalk. Headed home? To the beach too? The trees reached across the road, the leaves joining together to make an umbrella against the sun. Azaleas colored the ground, all pink and white and purple.

"I need to know about you," I said. "Tell me about you, Buddy." I stretched out my arms, still linked to him. My legs. My fingers. I even stretched out my hair. I kicked my feet in the garbage (McDonald's, Wendy's, and Taco Bell bags), trying to make a place to rest.

I needed to rest.

Maybe . . .

. . . maybe ghosts were allergic to the sun, and that meant I would never be able to go inside again because I had to avoid Tommie.

Buddy squeezed my fingers in his.

"Tell you about my life? What do you mean, Evie?"

We slowed and stopped for a red light. There was our town's cemetery. Would there be ghosts there? Waiting?

People who had drowned at the beach?

Car accident victims, waving?

Maybe only Tommie couldn't come outside.

Yup. There were aplenty in the cemetery. Standing under trees, mostly.

"You look so pretty breathing like that," Buddy said.

I tilted my head. "I always breathe like this," I said.

He nodded. "I know."

73

When we got to the beach, Buddy parked on the sand and rolled up his pants like guys in commercials about expensive perfume and sweaters do. He kept a tight hold on my hand, and the sun grew hotter by the water. Salt stuck to our lips and the sand got between our fingers. (Sand is magic. It finds its way into everything. Like ghosts.)

And I kept silent because the waves wanted me to sleep. I could tell by the way they rolled up onto my toes. And the sun wanted me to sleep and petted at my head, though I was sure I was getting a sunburn on my nose.

I just wanted to walk with this good-looking boy. I didn't need to know anything more about him and Tommie.

But that's not how life works.

Because as a couple of surfers were catching an okay wave, and three little kids ran into the water, their momma following them, and as I was getting ready to forget everything about everything, Buddy said,

"I loved Tommie."

74

"It was a long time ago."

"Who loves anyone at age twelve?"

"I did. We did."

Why had we walked so far? Now we had to go all the way back to the car that seemed to have made its way down to Cocoa Beach.

The wet sand shimmered. Foam drew lines in it, marking where the waves had ended.

My throat closed up.

Death played dirty tricks on the living. Yes, it did. Tragic, agonizing, deplorable tricks.

I spun around and looked into Buddy's face. He hovered right on the edge of another step, one that would push us together. He rocked in the wind, waiting.

"Never mind," I said, whispering. Somewhere down the beach a child screamed from joy.

I was kidding myself.

Why?

Because if his dead girlfriend wasn't in my bedroom when I went home this afternoon, would I have even cared if he had been in love?

No.

I would have been sad for him she was gone. But glad that I knew Buddy. And got to kiss him and look in those eyes of his.

He said, "I didn't think I'd ever want to be with someone else. But when I saw you . . ."

I shook my head. "I'm sorry." My words might have been carried away by the wind. And then, "When you saw me, what?"

Buddy looked at me so hard, something curdled in my chest. "I thought, 'That is the prettiest girl I have ever seen.' I was drooling all over myself. Then I thought, 'I'm ready to care about someone again.'" Waves crashed and a seagull cried out overhead. "You're different, Evie Messenger."

"You have no idea." I rested my head against his chest. That's what I needed. Him being ready for a new person in his life. Not sleep at all.

Buddy hugged me. "It's been a long time," he said. "I can talk about it now."

75

We talked in the car. He talked. Cried. I listened. Windows
down. Gusts of wind. Sand from my feet on the Wendy's bag
and black floor mat.

"I was there."

What? There?

He'd been *there*? In the car? In the wreck?

Jeez.

Jeez!

I sat quiet and listened.

But I couldn't help thinking maybe, maybe Buddy could
have died that day too.

"I walked away without a scratch."

"'Cause I had on my seat belt. And was in the back."

"Sometimes I still miss her. Tommie was funny."

"We talked about being together forever, and I never told
my friends 'cause they would have laughed."

"I thought she was terrific."

"Sometimes, when I glance at your bedroom window, I think I see her."

I twisted in my seat. Stared at Buddy.

"How do you know which room is mine?"

He sort of shrugged.

"I'm guessing. There're only four bedrooms in the house, and I thought . . ."

Nothing was mine alone.

"What?" he said. "I'm not a voyeur or anything. I mean, I'm not peeking in your window. I just guessed you'd have her room."

I swallowed. "I do."

He could see her. At my window. Or was it hers? I was confused.

"Don't look at me like that."

"Okay." I stared out my side of the car instead.

"No! You can look at me . . . just . . . damn it! Big deal! You have her room. I don't care. Even though I miss her. I'm . . . I'm glad you're here."

I let out a sigh of relief but kept staring outside the car.

"I tell you everything and I still can't say or do it right," Buddy said.

"What are you talking about?"

He shook his head. "Girls are so hard to figure out. Memories and the real thing."

Were we still arguing?

"Guys are the ones hard to figure out," I said.

But Buddy refused to even glance in my direction, so we drove the rest of the way home with not a sound but the traffic around us.

Yes, death plays dirty tricks on the living. And so do ghosts.

76

Buddy walked me to the front door.

"I hope," he said, looking somewhere near his feet, "you and me can be more than friends."

My stomach squeezed.

"I don't see why not," I said. But what I meant was, *I know your dead girlfriend and that could be a reason you and me can't be here together. 'Cause she's seen us at school and she might see us here at my house. Er. Her house. Uh. Whatever.*

Maybe we couldn't be together anywhere. What did I know?

"Really, Evie?" Buddy looked out from under his lashes.

"Really," I said. He looked so cute, staring at me that way. So cute, and a little sad. His eyes were so clear I could almost see myself in them. And that little pout . . . he leaned toward me . . .

"No!" I said, putting my hands against his chest. I felt his heart beating.

"What?"

"We can't . . . you know." I lowered my voice, glancing over my shoulder and then his. "Kiss. Out here."

Did Tommie watch from my bedroom—or was it her bedroom—right now?

"Why not? We have before. Wait. Did your parents see us?"

I shook my head.

"Then . . . what are you thinking?" Buddy looked serious. Like he really thought we could figure things out. But how can you do that with a ghost in the mix? "Do you want to give us time? Like to start over or something?"

A mockingbird cried out from a tree in the front yard. Aunt Odie drove past in slow motion. She gave the *I'm looking at you* hand signal. I shook my head at her. Gosh. There was no privacy from the living or the dead.

"I think," I said, pulling him by the hand, "we need to just go over to your place. Unless you and Tommie spent a lot of time there."

He nodded. "We did. My mom loved her too."

Well, then.

"Okay." I thought a moment. Aunt Odie's. I had to work there anyway. Had Tommie ever been down to her place before she died? Only one way to tell. "Come on."

77

"So what you're saying is, you don't know."

Buddy was long gone. After only one kiss—an almost-not-there kiss—a ghostlike kiss—on Aunt Odie's front porch.

"I'm scared of this one," he had said.

"My aunt?"

He nodded. I stood on tiptoe. Put my hands on his warm face.

"Bye, Evie."

Sheesh.

Now Aunt Odie shrugged. We stood in her kitchen, well-lighted from the sinking sun and all the bulbs burning.

"We never know," she said. "Part of the Gift is exploring what the Gift is to you."

I looked at her. I could smell dinner baking. Chicken and something spicy. Rolls, too. We would eat and then work until I had to get home and do homework.

"Lookit, I can't have ghosts showing up all the time," I said, like there was more than one. What would I do if *that* happened? If throngs of ghosts showed up on my doorstep? Like they did with Paulie. Or in my room like Tommie had. The thought was almost paralyzing.

"She's everywhere," I said. "And now this. Her boyfriend is the guy I like."

I gestured at the door as if Buddy stood there and hadn't gone on to his place.

"You like him?" Aunt Odie said. She grinned like she'd had something to do with us getting together.

I didn't answer.

Aunt Odie shrugged. She wiped her hands on her apron. "The call is different for us all. You happen to have a pretty amazing . . ." She glanced at the ceiling. Was she searching for the words up there? We were silent for a good minute.

This was embarrassing. My aunt couldn't even come up with a compliment *or* a criticism.

"Responsibility," she said at long last.

Okay then.

The timer went off. "Saved by the bell," she said.

I sat at the kitchen worktable, where I would soon be hand-packing Aunt Carolina's Parker House rolls. With love.

Aunt Odie scooped a huge portion of a cheesy meal onto a plate where angels flew around the border, dished up a side salad, and handed it to me.

"Say a prayer in your heart," she said, "blessing the food and this newest recipe."

I did while she got her own plate and Cokes for us both.

My aunt settled next to me with a bit of a groan. Her dress seemed to settle afterward. Then her hair. Like she was easing into place a bit at a time.

"What's important, Evie?"

Blowing on a strip of saucy chicken, a bit of chili pepper at the end, I glanced at her. "What do you mean?"

"What's it that you want in life?"

I popped the food into my mouth and chewed. My face turned pink.

Buddy.

No! He wasn't what I wanted for good. Was he? "Oh, you know. The usual."

Aunt Odie plowed into her salad. Nodded for me to continue.

"Do good in school. Go to college—for what, I have no idea. Meet a boy."

I hadn't thought about this before. Too many things had happened in the last couple of years. Things that kept me busy with life, living it, not worrying what I might do with it.

"That's all?"

Saying the words out loud made my sort-of plans feel rather vague. "There's more," I said. But I couldn't quite think of anything past true love and babies of my own in a house with a pool. Did I want to go to college? Build homes? Make baking mixes? Clean houses for other people? Do hair? I was confused.

"You used to know?" Aunt Odie ate good now. Dabbed at her lips with a real cloth napkin. A pearly-pink one.

"I'm not so sure." I slathered butter on the Parker House roll. Split it open and dabbed a dribble of honey in the middle. "Do I need to even know now, Aunt Odie? I want to . . . breathe. Take my time. Be a kid."

As soon as the words were out of my mouth, I knew it was true. I could wait one year. I could have one year to just have fun.

That seemed fair.

"I don't know about that. The Gift has come into your life, Evie. Things have changed for you."

My stomach seemed to fill on its own. I couldn't even take another bite. Was everything expanding in there?

"What do you mean?"

"I mean"—Aunt Odie waved her butter knife around—"I may be old, but when I turned fifteen, life changed forever for me. I was a water-skier, slalom. A champ. You know that. Had thoughts of being a professional."

This is true.

There's a picture of Aunt Odie, blown up to eleven by fourteen and hanging in the living room, of her skiing. She's bouncing over a wave. She's slender and her hair's pulled back in a ponytail and she's smiling—maybe even like life could never get any better than that.

She stood and went to the refrigerator to grab another

Coke. "I got a feeling I might need this. I don't usually eat food this spicy. Then"—Aunt Odie settled in her chair again, in layers—"I was dreaming food. Smelling it everywhere. Knowing the ingredients of things I tasted. The amounts. How to add them to the bowl. Everything changed. For the better, yes. Because I *let* that happen."

Wait. What? Really?

I swallowed. At nothing but spit. I should just lick at the butter and honey that melted and ran over my fingers. But my stomach refused.

"It took a little bit of time, but I figured out how to run my life and use the Gift at the same time. I suggest you do too, Evie. You can't fight it. It will eat you up. No pun intended."

78

Tommie was waiting when I got home. My food, untouched, filled the plastic Dixie plate.

"What do you mean?" she said before I had a chance to step all the way into the house. "What do you mean, I'm dead?"

I drew in breath.

I was wore out.

Too wore out for this.

But.

But if I paid attention to my Gift, it *might* go away. Aunt Odie had said as much. I just needed to be nice about it. Show some tact.

"I mean," I said. "You. Are. Dead." There.

I walked into the kitchen. In the family room I could hear the TV going. The news. Was Momma home? JimDaddy?

"That is so rude!" Tommie was hot on my heels. I could feel her close to my back. Her breath on my neck.

"Let me tell everyone I'm here," I said to Tommie, slapping

at her. She seemed ruffled, though nothing was out of place.

"That smells good," she said.

I set the plate on the counter.

"Have some." I walked out of the kitchen, past the formal dining room and down to the family room.

JimDaddy was propped up in a giant La-Z-Boy. Across the room, Momma and Baby Lucy were tucked into their own chair—not sharing with him like usual. My sister was sound asleep, her little mouth a perfect *O*.

"Hey, girl," JimDaddy said. "You still mad with me for not telling you everything?" He muted the TV.

"No, JimDaddy," I said. "Not mad at you, either, Momma."

The real word was "disappointed." But no need to say that. Kids can't let parents know when they don't act the way they should.

Momma reached her free hand up, and I leaned over so she could pet my face the way she always did before Jim-Daddy and Baby Lucy came along. "Love you." Her words were soft as her touch. I felt a bit of healing leave her fingertips. Sink into my skin and cool the frustration away some.

"You want I should put her down?" I asked.

Momma nodded.

I scooped Baby Lucy up. "I got homework and"—I paused and thought of Tommie waiting in the room down the hall—"stuff to do. Then I'm off to bed."

"Okay then," they said. Together.

"We'll be in a little later to say good night." Momma.

I walked out of the family room to my sister's room, where I lay Baby Lucy on her back. She let out a sigh. Then I was in the hall again, running my hand along the chair rail. My tennis shoes made squishy sounds on the marble. Wavering up ahead, outside my bedroom, I saw Tommie. She didn't look too happy.

I wasn't neither. So there.

I eased into my room, squeezing past her.

"I like your baby," she said.

I flopped on my bed.

"She sleeps in my momma's craft room."

Gulp.

Tommie sat down. The bed didn't even move under her weight. I scooted over.

"Why are you here?" I said.

"I live here."

I sat up. "Not anymore."

Tommie blinked. "Tell me about her."

"Who?"

"The baby."

"Baby Lucy," I said, "is Momma's dream. She never thought she could have another after I was born. Then a miracle." I remembered how excited Momma was when she found out. How she had Aunt Odie make a cake with the words WHAT ARE YOU EXPECTING? in pink and blue icing. It took

JimDaddy only a moment to know what Momma was trying to say.

I flopped onto my back again and stared at the ceiling.

"A baby with my daddy," Tommie whispered. She lay down next to me. Thank goodness I had a double bed or, well, this would be freaky. Lying in bed with a ghost. With a dead girl.

I nodded, all slow. Hadn't thought of that. Her dad and my mom. Me and Tommie, we were related by Baby Lucy. And our parents. We were an odd-shaped star fruit.

Tommie clasped her hands over her belly. I turned on my side to look at her. Her eyes were filled with tears. Outside of that barely-there smell, she seemed like anyone else.

Come to think of it, so did all those other dead people.

How did I know the difference between those who were alive and those who had passed on?

It was . . . a feeling. I mean, now that I knew what I was looking for, it was easy to see this was about the way I *felt*. Not about what I saw. Even though it *was* what I saw.

Too confusing.

"I was sure you were lying," she said. Her voice was a whisper.

"About what?" I tucked my pillow under my head better.

"About me. Being gone. Passed away. Up till now, I've just been . . . nowhere. In a dead space. . . ."

"What?"

"You know. Like that place before sleeping and dreaming."

"Oh."

The glow about her, pale pink, almost white, widened as she spoke.

"I remember the accident. I knew it was bad. Momma and me, we talked a moment or two after we crashed, and then there was a tap at Momma's window and some guy came to get us."

"Who?" I whispered the word.

"Some guy. He had this great smile. He told us to follow him. And I didn't go. I stayed behind. Watched my momma leave. I had Justin to stay back for. So I did. Then I was talking to you at your party."

Outside a bit of wind kicked up. Something tapped at *my* window. Another ghost? Probably. That was my luck.

"The dead spaces come when I'm all alone."

My heart was in my throat, like that old cliché says.

"At first I thought I was in the wrong place. But there was my daddy. He refused to see me. Only you would talk to me. And when you told me I was gone and I thought about not being able to turn on the water or the hand dryer . . ."

I didn't say anything. Because what do you say to a ghost who's just realizing she's dead? Dead but not quite gone.

When Tommie spoke next, her voice was almost not there. "Can you tell me what happened?"

And so I did. I told her about how JimDaddy still missed her and how he wished he had taken her to the picture show that day. I told her about the rain and that Buddy wasn't hurt, not physically anyway. I even told Tommie how Momma and JimDaddy had been seeing each other before she died. I told her everything, from start to finish, the best I knew how.

When I was done, it seemed Tommie had pretty much accepted my words as fact.

She was a ghost.

That light around her glowed so bright I wanted to ask her to leave the room and go sleep elsewhere.

But Tommie was crying.

So I let her stay with me.

79

You would think that a dead person would be satisfied to be hanging out.

No.

Tommie wanted more.

When JimDaddy and Momma came in to tell me good night, Tommie popped right up, wide-eyed, went straight over to her daddy, and slipped her arms around him. He started. Like he knew she was there. Then he leaned over and kissed me on the forehead.

"Night, girl," he said.

"That's what he used to say to me," Tommie said. She stood beside her father, watching him. "Look at me, Daddy," she whispered. And then, "He can't see me."

Momma plopped onto the bed where Tommie had lain. "You sleep good, sugar," she said.

"Okay." Maybe I would. If Tommie stopped her crying and went to sleep. Or whatever it was she did.

"Tell Daddy good night," Tommie said.

"What?" I said.

"I said sleep good," Momma said just as Tommie said, "Tell him!"

"No!" I said. Momma laughed and Tommie harrumphed.

"I mean, Momma," I said, sitting up in bed, "I mean yes, ma'am, I will."

Tommie got right in my face. "Do it," she whispered. "Do it." I could feel her breath on my ear. Sort of damp. Could smell that sour odor. "Please."

"Ummmm," I said.

JimDaddy stared at me. Ran his hands over his mouth. "For a minute you reminded me of my Tommie girl."

"Oh, Jim," Momma said. Only she didn't seem sad for him. She seemed, what? Frustrated?

Tommie was gone. Shimmered away and then back again, like a lightbulb deciding it had more strength than it thought.

In her room down the hall, Baby Lucy let out a sharp cry. A long, heartbroken wail followed. My heart stopped beating altogether, and when it started again, it felt like a pounding fist.

Momma, still looking unhappy with JimDaddy, patted my cheek. "I gotta get," she said. "See you in the morning."

"What did you do?" I said, leaping to my feet.

JimDaddy raised his hands.

"Nothing," he said. "It was just for a second. You reminded me of my little girl." He went to the door. "I better help your

210

momma with the baby. She might be more than one grown woman can take care of."

I wasn't sure if he meant Momma or Baby Lucy.

"Tell him!"

I spun around to face Tommie, then swung back to Jim-Daddy.

But he was gone.

"I said, what did you do?"

Tommie stood in the corner, arms folded across her chest. Her face looked sorta squished.

"Are you talking to me?" she said. Who knew a ghost could look smirky? I'm here to tell ya, they can.

"I told you to tell him something. You didn't. So *I* went to visit the baby."

I was to her in a moment. Across the wooden floor to the corner where the pink bled through the aqua-colored wall.

"You," I said. I raised a finger like I might poke her in the chest. But she was a ghost. And sure, I could feel her breath and talk to her and all that, but would my finger go through her or not? I didn't want to find out. "*You* stay away from my sister."

"She's my sister too," Tommie said. Her eyebrows went up and she tilted her head at me. "And what will you do if I *don't* stay away? Tell on me?" She suddenly looked like a ghost all right. Scary. Her eyebrows lowered into a scowl. Her eyes grew dark. "Kill me?" Her skin turned more pale, wispy, gray.

Okay, maybe she didn't look much different from a girl who had died and now stood in my bedroom, but jeez! Isn't that ghosty enough?

I swallowed. Clenched my hands into fists. Heard the blood in my ears. "You have no idea who you are dealing with."

"Oh? And who is that?"

We stood toe to toe.

"I am a Messenger," I said. "And I have powers."

Outside lightning cracked, lit up the sky. Thunder rumbled and the house shook.

"Seeing the dead is a power?" She said it like what *I* said was a joke.

It was a joke. What did I know about seeing the dead? Still, I tried. "You talking to anyone else?"

Lightning flashed again. Then rain pounded the roof like coins from heaven.

"Lots of people can see them, Evie. The Messengers don't have a corner on the market."

Others? Who cared about others? I cared about *us*. About my family.

"If you hurt my sister . . ."

There was another crash of thunder. Then, like it started, the rain stopped.

"Relax," Tommie said. It seemed the air slipped from

her body and she deflated. "I'm no demon. Babies can see me and . . . and . . . and they love me. When I was at the mall waiting for you to get back from wherever you and Justin went, I went around entertaining the masses. You took awhile, you know?"

Embarrassment tried to color my cheeks, but I refused to let it.

"Sorry," I said. "And the baby thing?"

I thought of my sister, all rosy and soft and sweet-smelling, having to sleep alone in her room. With a ghost about, no less.

Tommie slid over to where I was. "And nothing. Babies adore ghosts. Did she stare in the air and coo when she was younger?"

I nodded.

"Ghosts." Tommie looked off across the room. In the direction of Buddy's house. Her voice came out low. "I wanted babies of my own," she said. "With Justin." Then she looked at me.

I swallowed again.

A guilty swallow.

"Your sister cried because I *left* the room. Not because of anything else. I'm not evil. I don't even run with anyone evil. If I were to run at all."

"Oh," I said. Because what else do you say to a ghost who has a broken heart and is still in love with the guy you like?

That night after Tommie left, I imagined not getting babies you wanted, even if you were just twelve or thirteen.

I imagined leaving my momma and Baby Lucy and Aunt Odie—and JimDaddy, who was growing on me like mold.

What would I do without them?

If I left early?

If I left for good?

If anyone asks you if you want your Gift to be the one where you communicate with the dead—I mean full-on communicate— say no.

I wanted to be mad.

I wanted to make her leave and never see her again.

But I was the only one here for Tommie.

The only one who could see her and talk to her.

83

I wouldn't want that to happen to me.

    To lose everyone and everything.

    I sure would not.

Almost.

Almost asleep. Between awake and dreams.
Reaching for family. For before.
Reaching out.

85

In my dream there was the sound of a siren, wailing. Crying down the hall to the baby's room.

My feet had turned to wheels and I couldn't stand.

I jerked awake.

Silence blanketed my room, and out the front window I could see the moon, a saucer part full of cream.

86

The next morning, early, I rang Buddy's doorbell, checking over my shoulder every once in a while.

Did Tommie watch me?

The door opened and Buddy's momma (it had to be—she looked like a female version of him, only older . . . and meaner) stood there, hand on the knob.

She didn't say anything. Just stared at me. And waited. It was a long, cold minute.

"Ummm," I said.

She tilted her head.

"I . . ."

"Let me guess," Buddy's momma said. "You come for Justin Lee."

"Yes, ma'am."

"It's awful early, isn't it."

"Yes, ma'am."

"Six a.m."

"Yes, ma'am."

A breath of air swept down the street, damp as a wet wash-cloth. Storm clouds billowed out over the ocean. This sure was a wet fall.

"*Lots* of girls come looking for him."

"Oh." It was too humid out here. I wanted to adjust my clothing. Take off my bra and sling it back toward the house. Smooth my hair. Run, even. But I didn't. I stood there, muscles twitching.

"He's not here," she said. Her voice was low. Behind Mrs. McKay, in the massive foyer, I could see a painting of the family. There was Mrs. McKay, Mr. McKay (I supposed), and six boys, all of them different ages that looked like Buddy at different stages of life.

Buddy came down the hall then. For a moment it appeared he wore the massive chandelier as a crown. Then he saw me and headed toward the door, a huge smile on his face. He wore pajamas.

"Mom," he said, peering over the top of her head into my eyes.

She loosed the knob. Gave me one last stare.

"You can't do this anymore." Buddy towered over his momma. "She doesn't like that I date," he said, grinning.

I cleared my throat. Twice.

Mrs. McKay edged back to the staircase that ran like a cake decoration up to the second floor. She watched us until Buddy closed the door behind himself and me, with a click.

I let three minutes of used oxygen from my lungs.

"Wow," I said. "That was intense."

A redbird cried out and a mockingbird answered as Buddy grabbed my hand in his. "Not as bad as your aunt Odie." He grinned so big his eyes disappeared in their own squintiness. "Nice to see you, Evie."

"I don't think so," I said, and shook free. "Not here."

Who knew who was watching on either side of the street? Could be a ghost. Or an unhappy mother.

Buddy looked down at me.

"Five brothers?" I asked.

"Six," he said. "That portrait is old." He leaned toward me. I wanted to touch his arm. Smooth his hair.

But the living and the dead watched. (I could see his momma peering out the glass now. Staring at us. She wagged her finger at me.)

I pulled away. "I need a ride," I said. "Can you help me?"

Buddy nodded. "Sure. Let me change my clothes."

87

I held Buddy's hand all the way outta New Smyrna.

We kissed at each red light.

Cassadaga came into view far too soon.

What was it with the weather?

Billowy clouds had turned gray. Dark. Ready to let loose.

"We're looking for . . ." I kept my eyes peeled on the side of the road, searching for Paulie's place.

Cassadaga seemed different at the crack of dawn, with the storm moving in, not right on top of us.

At first I could see, though the air darkened and grew thicker. Buddy turned on the windshield wipers even though it wasn't raining.

A slow fog drifted close to the road. Across it. Into the woods.

The sky looked like an eggplant.

Buddy turned loose of my hand.

Flicked on the headlights.

Watched the road.

Until, "That's his place right there," I said.

Paulie rolled his eyes when he opened the door. I could see by his face we had awakened him.

"What?" I said. Behind him the dead lingered, wandered, stared off into space.

"Not you again. And without your aunt *or* an appointment. This is too early for no appointment."

"Lookit," I said. Buddy stood so close, he kept bumping into me. "If you can tell the future, you shoulda known I was coming."

Paulie blocked the door. "I don't tell the future. That's William down the road a piece."

I pushed my way past Paulie, wishing for Aunt Odie but knowing I had to do this on my own. "'Scuse me," I said to several spirits, who parted and let me come in the front room.

"I'm Buddy," Buddy said, and he reached to shake hands with Paulie.

Paulie raised his fingertips like he had gotten his nails done.

"Can't touch anyone until the right time," he said. His voice was almost an apology.

Buddy glanced at me. "O-kay," he said.

Paulie closed the door behind us. The house went dark, dark, dark.

"You need a reading?" he said. But not with much oomph. He gestured toward the table.

"I need answers," I said.

Paulie drew himself up tall. There was a nervous look around his eyes. "What makes you think I have answers?"

I glanced at the room. The curtains pulled open at the front windows were purple paint color. The same shade of purple as in Paulie's billowy housecoat.

We stood there.

Toe to tippy-toe.

Me glaring up.

Him gawking down at me.

When I checked on Buddy, I saw that not one ghost was interested in him. He sat at the edge of the sofa, and all today's visitors (or were they here always, waiting, hoping for someone to drop in and ask about them?) had moved away and crowded closer to me and Paulie. Like they listened to us.

"You know something." I whispered the words.

He didn't move. Didn't blink. Didn't even seem to breathe.

"You knew on my birthday."

Still nothing.

"I heard you. I heard Aunt Odie. There's something going on, and I need to know what it is."

Paulie came to life then. Swept one hand at Buddy, pointing his way to the sofa (and dark-cherry-colored divan), then toward a door where I read the words NO ADMITTANCE.

90

Considering the storm brewing outside, the back part of Paulie's house was bright as sunshine. The walls in the kitchen were yellow, the appliances were stark white, the sink deep and filled with fresh-cut flowers standing in water.

There were no ghosts.

"Wow," I said.

"Working with darkness, you stay in the dark." Paulie put a teakettle on. "Got some of your auntie's chamomile tea here. I do not know how she makes it."

"With love," I said.

Paulie smacked his lips. "That is the truth," he said. "I can taste it. You wanna cup too?"

I nodded. "Sure," I said, settling onto a chair the color of limes. "But you know what else I want."

Sigh. "Answers."

91

"We each got something," Paulie said. He raised and lowered the tea bag. "We come with it. All of us. The Gift, as your family says."

So Tommie was right.

I sipped at my drink, almost too hot, that Paulie had added honey to.

Nodded. This I had heard.

"It's like a light, for most. Some? They never know they even have a Gift. Then there are people like me. A guide of sorts." He pressed his thumbs to his chest. "I can help you see what you have. There are those people like your aunt." He waved his hand. "She has a Gift that's bigger. People might call it magic. But you and I know better."

I held my breath.

I knew it.

I felt empty. Hollow. Waiting.

Scared?

No. Nervous.

"So your auntie, she's a good woman, isn't she?" Paulie handed me a macadamia nut cookie and took one for himself. "Made with love," he whispered as he took a bite. Crumbs fell onto the table, and he wet his finger and ate them up. "She has a different degree of seeing. She can taste what a spirit offers her. Sees the words plain and clear."

I thought of the recipes that came to Aunt Odie.

"I'm a psychic. I been helping your family for years. Years and years. Find their specialties."

"Years?"

"Much longer than you can believe."

We stared at each other.

"*Much* longer."

I gulped.

"Oh."

"And I help others, too. It's my *job*. Get thoughts and feelings from the dead sometimes to give advice to the living." Paulie looked at me. "But you, Evie. You are different. You have a big power. You see the dead. Converse with them, maybe." He glanced at me.

He tapped the table with his fingernails.

I nodded. Gulped again. Tried to breathe. Whispered, "Yes."

"Evie, look. I feel it's even more than that. Your duties might be a little more complicated. But am I right? About the conversing?"

My voice warbled from me, like a dying bird might sound. "I can see them. Lots of them here in Cassadaga. Your place is crawling with them."

Paulie tilted his head.

"Crawling?" he asked.

"Crawling."

"That's how you knew about Ezra Bargio."

I nodded. "The woman—his sister—wanted him to know everything was okay. She practically forced me to tell."

He glanced around the spotless kitchen. "Crawling?" he asked again.

"And I see her."

Paulie shivered like a goose—or a ghost—had run over his grave.

"This one girl. I talk to her. She follows me. Always there. Maybe like the people in the other room."

Paulie's eyes were wide as pies.

"They're friendly," I said.

He swallowed. "You sure? Sometimes a 'force' will come that's ugly. I have to send it away."

Now I nodded. "But lookit. *I* need help."

"Of course." Paulie held his hands out, palms up. An uneaten cookie sat there. Who had handed it to him? "I knew what you could do when you were here. It's been a long time since someone like you has come into your family. I was surprised." He coughed, and a cookie crumb flew from his mouth. It landed on the tabletop, but Paulie didn't go after that morsel. "You sure they're friendly?" he asked.

"I'm sure."

Paulie ate the remaining cookie in two bites. Was he making me wait on purpose? "Now you have to understand something."

"Okay." That's why I was here. To understand. If I could catch my breath. And if Paulie could just catch his.

"Your aunt didn't come on her Gift all at once. Neither did I. We searched it out. Figured it out. Figured what there was that had to be done. Now the Gift must be right at the top of your most-important list. You have to take care of it. Not just keep your name when you marry."

"Are you saying," I said, "I don't *have* to be like this?"

"Huh?" Paulie said.

"Are you saying I could leave this behind?"

"Oh, I wouldn't do that."

"Why not? You got a room full of ghosts waiting on you. I don't want that. Right now I got one who climbs in my bed."

"That's scary," Paulie said. He shivered.

"You're telling me."

Paulie took my hand in his. "They won't go just because you want them to. Just because you ignore them."

"Answer this for me. Can I lose this Gift, Paulie?"

He hesitated. Made an expression like he hadn't heard what I said.

"Can I?"

"Well, sure, Evie. A person can lose anything."

That was all I needed.

I leaned back in the chair. My tea had cooled. Outside the window the rain fell. Heavy, fat drops that left the heavens in slow motion, like they might change their minds and head back to where they had come from. Maybe because, at last, I had an answer I could tolerate.

92

Well, well, well.

    I didn't have to do this.

    I could ignore it.

    If I wanted.

    Or train my mind to the Gift.

    If I wanted.

    And I didn't.

93

It wasn't my responsibility to take care of Tommie. No matter what I'd thought.

Someone else could do it.

94

"Kiss me here, before we get to school," I said. I needed to get rid of this ghost feeling. Get rid of this *I'm responsible* feeling.

Buddy didn't even hesitate. He pulled the car over to the side of the road. "Here?" he said, shutting off the engine.

We were a good ways out of Cassadaga.

I could taste the flowery chamomile still. "We don't want anyone watching us," I said as I leaned over the emergency brake to him.

"Right," he said. His lips touched mine. "Mmmm, sweet."

"Thank you."

Then Buddy pulled away. "What do you mean, anyone watching us? We don't do PDA. I believe in keeping what's important to me all my own."

"What?" I said, my voice going all screechy.

He smiled at me.

For a moment I forgot where I was. I was that comfortable. "Evie."

The windows steamed up. Expect Florida weather to get

things steamy before they even have a chance to on their own.

"What?"

"What makes you think people been watching us kiss?"

I looked out the window.

No ghosts. No Tommie. I shrugged.

"It's your dad, isn't it? Your JimDaddy." Buddy took a tight hold of the wheel.

"What? Gross. Are you kidding me? No. Ick."

Buddy ran his hands around the steering wheel. He sure looked cute when he was bothered. I let down my window to get a bit of cooler air in the car. A mosquito buzzed in. I killed it.

"He used to watch me and Tommie."

I raised my eyebrows. Folded my hands in my lap. "Watch you? Like *watch* watch you?"

"Like 'I'm a father and I have my eye on you' watch us."

"I see."

Buddy started the car. "You know," he said, switching the car into gear. "It's been years. I'd like to move on. But there are so many reminders."

He pulled out in the street without even looking in the rearview mirror.

Whoever was in the car behind us laid on the horn, and Buddy flipped him off out the back window. Not that anyone could see from the steam. "We gotta get to class," he said.

95

So maybe I had decided I would ignore my ghosty seeing abilities.

Maybe I had decided I would *not* perfect them.

Maybe I had decided I would *not* let Tommie enter my head again, because that's where I wanted my momma to be. And my little sister. And my aunt and almost-boyfriend and my stepfather.

Just no Tommie.

So why was she in my mind?

I would have to work harder.

96

Tommie waited at the double doors at the school. Glared at me and Buddy, drifted behind, on my heels.

"If I could," Tommie said, "I'd appear right now and make Justin see me."

I said nothing.

"Remind him of us together."

I flapped my hand at her in a *go away* way.

"He was mine first."

Buddy walked inside the school, like it wasn't even raining. Tall and beautiful and anxious and worried and how could he be so cute and I liked him and wanted to be with him and there he was, opening the door for me, then saying, "See ya, Evie," and leaving me standing there, rain spattered.

He didn't even look me in the eye.

I watched Buddy take off down the hall. Kelly zoomed out of nowhere, swinging up next to him. He said something to her. I saw his mouth move. That mouth I'd just kissed. They walked away together. He didn't turn. Didn't wave.

I gulped.

Were we done? The two of us? Done because of Jim-Daddy?

Did Tommie have something to do with this?

My stomach clenched and my hair felt damp. I could tell it had gone frizzy. I . . . I wanted to weep.

I wiped at the water on my face. Fanned my T-shirt. My throat felt tight.

Tommie came closer. "You two are late." She checked her wrist as if she wore a watch.

"Did you make him leave?" I said.

"I wish."

"Tommie," I said. "I like him."

Her face grew tense. "I did too. I *loved* him."

"Now he's with . . ."

"That awful Kelly. She went to school with him from sixth grade on."

All around us people hurried. They hollered and laughed and kissed and squealed and swore and fought. Bumping into me. Walking through Tommie, who shivered each time it happened.

My heart pounded.

I would ignore her. I had to. I needed my simple life back.

Make her go away for good.

"You *can't* make me go away," she said.

I bit at my lip.

I clipped down the hall to the first restroom I could find, the teachers' lounge. I would blow-dry my shirt and pull my hair into a braid or something. Knot it. Chop it off.

Why couldn't I have Aunt Carol's skill at hair design?

Why did I have to have *this* Gift?

I kept up my planning. I would hide till school was over (maybe not in the lounge but some other bathroom), then walk home.

The smell of cigarette smoke assaulted me when I stepped in the lounge. This room was too small for smoking, with a couple of sofas and a microwave and way over that way, the restroom door.

"I see you. You see me."

Tommie was there. Arms folded. Legs crossed at the ankles.

The room was empty. Well, you know. Except . . . I skittered across the floor, quick, so a teacher wouldn't see me in here, and ran into the bathroom.

Keep calm, Evie. Have a backbone. Resolve not to use the Gift.

"Get going," I said to my reflection. I locked the door.

Tommie pushed through the wood.

I turned on the hand dryer. The rain splotches weren't that bad. Tears dripped on my shirt, matching the droplets of rain.

Tommie scooted closer. The hot air rippled through her, but she didn't seem to notice. This was my first indication

Tommie wasn't real. And the door thing, which I hadn't seen until this very minute.

"Why are you crying?" she asked. Her voice was tender. She put her hand on my shoulder, and my skin tingled under hers. "Oh! I can touch you."

I shook my head. I couldn't say, *You know that boy you left behind? I like him more than you know. And now he's dumped me.*

So instead I said, "Go."

"You're too late," Tommie said. Her face was dead serious. No pun intended. "You and I have bonded. We're inseparable."

"Paulie said—"

"He's wrong. I'm here for good."

The tears dried up and a bit of Messenger steel went down my spine.

"We'll see about that," I said.

97

In biology, the long test tubes on each table. People wearing safety goggles. Me partnered with Jo Dorman. Bunsen burners.

"I'm here."

98

The gym, where we all stood as spots and Vicki Finlay jumped on the trampoline and then without warning rolled right off—midleap—and onto the floor.

"I'm here."

99

Even in the lunchroom, where the Sloppy Joes, made with soy protein and a little beef, stained the plastic plates a greasy orange. Aunt Odie would have been disgusted. I sure was, and I wasn't even eating this crap. My lunch had been packed by a pro.

"I'm here."

100

Me: Please. Go away.

Tommie:

101

That night.

Late.

After I cried for twenty minutes in the shower . . .

After I helped with dinner and Baby Lucy and watched Momma and JimDaddy sitting apart on the sofa when we should have all been watching *Hook*, one of JimDaddy's favorite movies of all time . . .

After I had walked to my aunt's house and let her try to hug and feed my sadness away . . .

I went to bed.

The house was silent, and I hadn't seen Tommie for hours. Was she gone? I flipped off the light and snuggled myself into bed, thinking maybe, maybe I was free, maybe all I had to do was ask her to go and she would.

So why was I sad? This was what I wanted.

Today was too long. Too gloomy. I'd lost Buddy and Tommie and there was weird stuff going on with JimDaddy and Momma. Their relationship. I couldn't ignore it anymore. I couldn't ignore any of this. My cells ached and I was sure it was because the Gift pulled at them, trying to make me do what it thought I was supposed to do.

Tommie's face materialized next to mine on my pillow.

"We're friends," she whispered.

I drifted off toward sleep.

An ache filled my heart and I knew what I had to do, because what would it be like to be *all* alone?

102

And in my heart I knew I was a Messenger, through and through.

103

Shhh. You sleep. You rest.
Everything will be okay.

104

"Look," I said to Aunt Odie the next afternoon. I'd come to her place like she asked.

She stared in my eyeballs.

I sifted flour and baking powder together. Then salt.

"Are you thinking loving thoughts?" Aunt Odie said. Behind her the sun broke through the window and crowned my aunt with a halo.

"Not really." I knew what was coming.

"Then you can't work on the food."

Aunt Odie waited until I said, "Fine."

I clapped my hands free of ingredients. Flour poofed in the air like a cloud. "I better stop working."

"Yes, you better had. You know what makes this product the best in the land."

"Love," we said at the same time.

I pulled the apron over my head and threw it on the table (with no love), then stomped around the kitchen like I might make an exit any second (also with no love). Aunt Odie took my hand. Led me into the living room. She plopped down in a rocker in a dusty puff.

"Climb on up onto my lap," she said. She patted her knees. "You know I will hold you long as your feet don't touch the floor."

I gave a bit of a nod. Only a woman who dreamed recipes and was assisted in the creative cooking process by the dead would hold me, no matter that I was taller than her, no matter if her own feet had a hard time reaching the floor when she sat in the rocker.

Aunt Odie's been saying I can sit on her lap since I can remember. Maybe even longer. I bet she said that to me first thing, right after I was born and she held me in her arms that early morning when it rained so hard and the weather was so rough three tornadoes were spawned. She probably said these words, "I'll hold you on my lap as long as your feet don't touch the floor," 'cause her momma said it to her and her grand-mother before that and her great-grandmother—you get the picture.

In slow motion, I walked to where Aunt Odie sat. I eased myself onto her lap. Pulled my feet up so not even my toes would touch the flowered carpet.

The rocker moved and I let out a sigh. No matter what anyone says, fifteen is not too old to have your auntie hold you and soothe away the rumples that ghosts can cause. And boys. And parents, too.

"This is the way of the Messengers," she said.

"Yes, ma'am." I whispered my answer.

Outside, far away, I heard a siren go off and a dog howled.

"There's a reason you are the way you are, Evie," Aunt Odie said after a few minutes of rocking. The words came out like a new song. "A reason I am the way I am. A reason everyone is the way they are. We each got duties. Some are easier known for a few of us. Like you and me. We're lucky. We *know* what we are called for here on earth. Some people go through trials doing this, that, and the other thing trying to settle on what they're supposed to do here in life. And some don't find out till they have gone from this life to the next. When it's too late. And then maybe they have wasted their chance at serving others and making the world a better place." She let out a long sigh, like air being released from a balloon. "You should be glad about that, Evie. That you know."

I didn't answer, but I thought.

Maybe I didn't *want* to help others.

Maybe I didn't *want* to leave the world a better place.

I rolled my eyes at myself. Of course I did.

Aunt Odie was right.

At least, that's the way I felt as she rocked me till the sun slipped away and all the world was covered with an evening blanket and I needed to get home so I could hold my baby sister, tight, on my own lap.

Before I left her place, Aunt Odie patted my shoulder,

handed me a casserole dish that was steaming hot, and said, "Listen, shug. I think they need to tell you what's going on down to your place."

I narrowed my eyes at my aunt. "What are you saying?"

Aunt Odie shifted from one foot to the other.

"It's your momma," she said after a long minute.

105

I ran the whole way home, casserole dish in front of me like a gift from one of the Three Wise Men. When had eight houses gotten to be such a distance? And what was wrong with Momma? Was she sick? Dying?

"No, no, no," I said.

"Evie," Buddy hollered. Then he was jogging beside me. "I been thinking about us." The evening was a sepia-colored photograph, tinged blue.

Oh great.

"You want I should help you with that?" He reached for the casserole dish.

I shook my head.

He said, "I wonder if maybe . . . maybe we're moving too fast."

I swallowed. Tears sprang to my eyes. "I gotta get to my momma."

Then I jogged off, leaving Buddy behind, up my sidewalk and into the house.

106

I stood in the foyer, the chandelier sparkling, scattering fairy light everywhere.

"Where you been?" Tommie said. "Things are happening here."

I clomped into the kitchen.

Had Buddy just broken up with me? And the two of us not even dating?

I grabbed a rooster oven mitt and set the dish on it, then swung around to meet Tommie. She was nose to nose with me. I took a step backward.

"Personal space," I said.

"That smells real good." Tommie breathed in deep, closing her eyes.

"It's made with—"

"Love," JimDaddy said. He stood in the doorway. "Who you talking to, Evie?" His voice wasn't more than a whisper. And had he . . . I looked closer . . . had he been crying?

What should I do with my hands?

And my words?

What should I say?

"Tell him," Tommie said. "Tell him I'm here."

Momma appeared behind JimDaddy before I could speak, and it was clear she was in no mood to be messed with. You know those old cartoons that show smoke rising from a character's ears? That was my mother now.

"What's going on here?" I said, like I was the parent.

Baby Lucy came into the kitchen next. Scooting. She flumped on her bottom to sit herself up and grinned. I could see a bit of one tooth showing through her gums.

My mother and stepfather were silent. Not acknowledging each other.

Baby Lucy crawled over to Tommie and cooed at her.

Tommie grinned. Twisted a baby curl around her ghost finger.

"I been cleaning all day," Momma said, "and your Jim-Daddy here come home and plopped on the bed like I hadn't just made it."

We all looked at him. Even Baby Lucy. And Tommie.

JimDaddy didn't say anything, just sank into a chair.

"I been watching your sister." Momma looked burnt around the edges.

I wasn't sure what to say.

JimDaddy let out a huge sigh. A big, huge, gigantic sigh.

"Tell him I'm near," Tommie said. She'd drifted to him when I wasn't paying attention.

"She's mad at me 'cause of me missing the girls," Jim-Daddy said.

If he woulda shouted at me, I wouldn't have been more shocked.

"Your girls?"

"Is he . . . ," Tommie asked. "Is he talking about me?"

"Are you talking about . . ."

"His family what passed on," Momma said. She got this funny look on her face like maybe she understood just how bad that sounded.

"I can't get away from the sadness," JimDaddy said.

Momma didn't say anything and neither did I.

"Daddy," Tommie said. "Daddy."

She slid to her father, and Baby Lucy watched Tommie go.

"I don't mean to feel this way," JimDaddy said.

And Momma said, "Jim, I know that. I understand losing the love of your life. I get it. But you close up when you start your mourning. And the mourning's been going on since we started dating. I can handle being in second place. But you're cold to me. You ignore me. That's what I can't bear." Her voice was like melted chocolate, so soft and velvety and kind. Plus sad. Momma, I could see, was sad too.

She laid a hand on his shoulder. "You gotta let me in," she said.

But JimDaddy, he didn't say anything. Not one word at all.

107

"She's here," I said. "She's been here since my birthday."

Momma and JimDaddy stood silent. Had they heard?

"Tommie's here. Right this second."

JimDaddy shifted.

Momma took a step. Then another.

"It's my Gift. I see dead people. And talk to them. At least this one." I remembered the woman at Paulie's. "And one more. So at least two."

Now JimDaddy looked at me. Then at Momma. Then at me again.

"I thought your Gift hadn't manifested itself," Momma said. She wore this expression like she wasn't sure if she should laugh or cry.

"Oh, it's here," I said.

"What's here?" JimDaddy.

"The Gift," me and Momma said at the same time.

"Dead people," I said.

"Huh?" he said.

"When?" Momma asked.

"I told you." My voice was a sigh.

"That's right," Tommie said, but of course, no one heard her. Except Baby Lucy, who crowed with pleasure.

"Are you kidding?" Momma raised her eyebrows.

"I wish I was."

"I am so proud of you, honey. I get planning things. Aunt Odie gets cooking. Carol gets hair. And you . . ." She kissed my face. "Your kind are few and far between."

I gave Momma a death glare. "What? You think I wanted this?"

Everyone was quiet except Tommie. "So this is what you get to experience when you tell people about me."

Baby Lucy clapped and let out a bubble of laughter.

This wasn't funny at all.

JimDaddy ran his hand over his face. "You Messengers are something else," he said.

"You believe me?"

"Why shouldn't he?" Momma said.

I tilted my head at her. "Are you really asking me that?"

"He's used to us," she said.

The doorbell sounded, but no one moved except Tommie, who said, "It's Justin. *And* your aunt."

"Why didn't you say something sooner?" JimDaddy said.

I shrugged. "I didn't know at first. I sorta just figured it out myself. Plus, it's been less than a week."

"Want me to get the door?" Tommie asked.

I looked to where Tommie stood. She glowed. Like something from a movie.

"Stop that," I said. "And no. Aunt Odie will let herself in." But what about Buddy? I gulped, wanting to choke on nerves.

"Are you . . ." JimDaddy didn't stand up all the way. He was a hunchback version of himself. "Are you talking to her now? Is she here now?"

Tommie stood right next to her daddy.

"Yes, sir," I said.

The doorbell sounded again.

"What's she doing?" JimDaddy said.

"Acting up."

JimDaddy's voice caught in his throat. He took a deep breath. "She always did joke around."

Momma hadn't moved. Baby Lucy crawled over to Tommie's feet, and Tommie sat so my sister could get closer to her.

"I shoulda died too. That day," JimDaddy said.

"Jimmy," Momma said. My stomach tightened.

But JimDaddy didn't look at Momma. I could see how she wanted him to. How she needed him to . . . I don't know what. Include her in his grief? I wasn't sure. It was awful watching the two of them.

"She wanted to go to the show. Tommie wanted to see some movie about true love. She went with her momma."

"Daddy?" Tommie said, but of course he didn't hear her.

JimDaddy stared off at nothing, it seemed. Off over my head. Maybe through the wall, maybe to Daytona half an hour away, maybe all the way to New York City, where he and Momma took their honeymoon right after getting married till death do us part.

"Daddy?"

"So they went. And I stayed. Drove off to work, and on the way back home I passed the fire trucks and the police and the ambulances."

"Jim," Momma said.

I tried to clear my throat. Tried not to hear his sorrow. Not to see it. But it was all over his face. It dripped off him and splashed onto the floor.

"I pushed past everyone. Shoved an EMT to the ground. Ran to the car window."

"I'm here," Tommie said.

"Tried to open the door, get my baby out. Slammed my hands on the glass. But they were gone."

"Honey," Momma said. "Listen."

"A father should protect his family." He ran his hands over his face. "When they let me touch her, hold her close, when I told her good-bye . . ." He stopped speaking. "I was covered with her blood and I had no idea. Not for hours."

It felt like the room was a terrible scene in a movie. Only worse. Way worse.

"You know what's strange?" JimDaddy asked, and Momma shook her head. "That I knew soon as I saw the fire engine. I knew. As if one of them whispered the whole accident in my ear."

"Wait," Tommie said. "I did that." I could tell she was remembering the experience all the sudden. "I—I told him so he would know." She looked at me wide-eyed. Touched her fingers to her lips. Baby Lucy let out an ear-piercing wail, like she'd been stung by a bee. "I wanted him to know we were gone. Wanted him to know I didn't blame him. And that I loved him."

"You told me, Jim," Momma said. But he didn't seem to hear her. "Jim, I'm right here for you. Right here."

I looked at Momma weeping.

At Tommie and Baby Lucy, crying too.

At JimDaddy, whose eyes had filled with tears.

"Jimmy," Momma said.

And when JimDaddy didn't even look at her, she said, "If there is anything the Messengers know, it's that you cannot compete with the dead. I have tried and tried to help with your healing, Jim. But I'm done." And she left the room, called for Aunt Odie to come on in, then ran off, light-footed, down the hall.

108

"All hell's broke loose," Aunt Odie said.

"Evie," Buddy said, "I didn't mean I was worried about us going fast. I've thought it over. I like things fast."

"Ain't no one who can compete with the dead," Momma said.

"Why, why, why?" JimDaddy said. Tommie hovered near him.

Baby Lucy sounded like a tornado siren.

I was in a blender of people, alive and dead, heartbroken and happy, good-looking and rich.

No wonder Paulie had closing hours! No wonder.

I wiped my eyes and followed the most important problem down the hall.

109

"Where are you going?"

Momma still cried, but she didn't answer. She stumbled into Baby Lucy's room and pulled out an unopened package of Huggies and a few sleepers, onesies, and other clothes for my sister.

My stomach fell to the balls of my feet.

"What are you doing?" My voice took a swipe at the light dangling all pretty and sweet with pink crystal baubles.

Momma swung around, fast. Her eyes were huge. Her face matched the color of the chandelier, like she'd been turned into a porcelain doll.

"What does it look like?" she said between the crying hiccups. Her hair trembled.

"Umm," I said, and took a step back.

"Go get packed."

"What?"

"Now." Then she pushed past and into the hall and headed toward the master bedroom. That would slow her down for sure. I mean if Momma was gonna look through all her things, jeezo peezo, she had a week's worth of work, at least.

I followed on tiptoe, panting from nerves. Why, I might be the first girl who sees ghosts to die of a heart attack—or deoxygenation—at the age of fifteen.

That didn't seem right either. Nothing did.

"Momma? Momma? Momma?" I whispered after her the whole way. My hands flapped like I hoped to take off in flight and land in front of her. I was getting ready to say, *You got your work cut out for you, and that's good, Momma, 'cause then you'll have some time to think over what you are about to do*, when she threw open her closet door, walked in, and stepped out with a roll-y suitcase. Bulging. Packed.

There was a huge commotion going on at the front of the house. I could hear Buddy, Aunt Odie, and Tommie arguing. I gaped at my mother.

"What's that?" I pointed at the suitcase.

"For someone who can see ghosts and talk to dead people and who has a sixth sense, you aren't catching on to things all that quick."

Momma had stopped crying. In fact, she now appeared angry.

I drew my head back like a turtle trying to hide in its shell.

"That was not nice," I said, my feelings hurt. "I can see *what* it is. I'm not dumb." Though I felt that way. "And you *know* what I mean, anyway."

"Be on my side," she said.

"I'm *always* on your side." I looked at her. And the suitcase. And the things she threw on her bed while I flitted around in the room.

"Why are you doing this?" I had a hard time getting the words out. They didn't want to, 'cause anyone or anything with a sixth sense or not could see where this disaster was headed.

"I'm leaving." She opened the suitcase, the zipper singing.

"But why?"

Momma crammed Baby Lucy's things on top of her own stuff. Including, I saw, the picture Momma and JimDaddy had made when they got engaged.

"You love each other."

"I know that. I love him more than my own life." Momma's hands trembled. "But love isn't everything."

What? Really? Wasn't there a million famous songs saying love *was* all you needed? Didn't JimDaddy sing a lot of them? To my mother? With his guitar?

Standing there in that fancy bedroom, I realized Jim-Daddy hadn't sung once in the few days since my party. Not once. Not to Momma. Or Baby Lucy. And he used to all the time.

JimDaddy had asked her to marry him with a song.

Was this why Momma was done?

The suitcase looked like it was ready to bust wide open when Momma closed it. Well, she sorta closed it. The diapers were never going in there. And a onesie had stopped the zipper. Plus a sleeper foot hung out the opening, too.

"I thought—"

"Don't you say a word." Momma swiped at her tears. "I have lived with this since long before me and Jim got married." She stopped, and I wondered if Momma was thinking about the county courthouse and how afterward Aunt Odie had served Better than Sex Cake and said to all the guests, "Good marriages are death do you part, but the lucky ones stay together longer than that. The good ones," Aunt Odie had said, "stay together forever. Long past death."

What would Aunt Odie think of this?

"We're off to Aunt Odie's," Momma said. "The three of us. You included."

Wait. Wait!

"I don't think—"

"She knows we're coming."

"That's obvious." I said the words under my breath but where I knew Momma could hear me. Then I stopped her from leaving her room, hands gripping her elbows, leaning in to keep her from moving.

I said, "Momma. This doesn't feel right," just as there was another knock at the front door.

110

"Anyone gonna get that?" I hollered when the knock sounded again.

Momma sat on the bed, defeated.

"Wait a minute," I said. "Let's wait and see what we can talk out."

Momma's eyes were shiny. I could see that sadness all over her.

Like with JimDaddy.

I ran down the hall, ran past everyone. Aunt Odie was in the kitchen, tinkering with something and holding Baby Lucy in one arm. "The door," I said to her, and she looked at me like someone from a dream.

Tommie floated around her father, who sat on his recliner. Not all relaxed, but head in hands. "I can do it," he was saying. "I can do it."

"The door," I said, but no one answered.

There in the foyer was Buddy.

"Evie," he said. "Lookit. I wanna talk to you."

I tilted my head at him. "Why didn't *you* open the door?"

He shrugged. "It's not my house."

The knock sounded again.

I unlocked the door and threw it open wide.

"Paulie!" I said.

111

"Oh, hey," Buddy said, and reached to shake Paulie's hand, but Paulie raised them and said, "Not ready. Not ready." And to me, "May I?"

I think I'd swallowed my tongue. When I found it, I said, "What are *you* doing here?"

"Come to help," he said. "If you'll allow it."

Aunt Odie hurried into the foyer. "My favorite man, Paulie," she said. Joy was written all over her face. Baby Lucy clapped.

They smiled pretty at each other. What was this? Another love story?

"Come on in," I said.

Paulie was so tall I wondered if he could touch the two-story ceiling in here. His dark skin was beautiful.

"Come sit down," I said.

Me and Paulie and Buddy and Aunt Odie and Baby Lucy, bunched like we were all joined at the hip, moved to the living room.

JimDaddy looked up.

Momma was in here now, sitting across the room from her husband. When had she sneaked in?

Tommie sat next to her father. She leaned against him, head on his arm.

"Oh my," Tommie said as Paulie staggered and fell to his knees.

112

"Paulie," Aunt Odie said, setting Baby Lucy on the sofa. "Paulie!"

"What's going on?" Momma said.

"Call 9-1-1," Buddy said, and he pulled his phone out, nearly dropping it.

"Do you need help?" JimDaddy asked. In four giant steps he stood next to Paulie.

"I'm fine, I'm fine," Paulie said. "I wasn't expecting . . ."

Tommie was next to me and Paulie now.

"I know you," Tommie said.

"Why are you here?" Paulie gulped. "I thought . . . I thought I helped you pass over?"

"Huh?" I said. "You what?"

"I was there with her," Paulie said, and then to Tommie, "With you."

"I remember," Tommie said. She came closer to Paulie. Put her arms around his neck. He didn't protest.

"What's going on?" JimDaddy said.

"Paulie's talking to Tommie," I said.

"What went wrong?" Paulie said. "She shouldn't be here." He asked like I might know the answer.

My eyes went wide. "I have no idea."

"Where's my girl?" JimDaddy said.

"Tommie?" Buddy said. "Tommie's here? Are you kidding? What the hell is going on?"

"I want to tell her good-bye," JimDaddy said. "Properly." The room felt hot as an oven.

Aunt Odie moved around, smells of cookies and gingerbread and vanilla pudding floating around her. "Oh," she said. "Oh, oh, oh. This has never happened with the Messengers."

Paulie gave her a dirty look.

Baby Lucy smiled at everyone, everything, cooing.

"What is going on?" Buddy said. "How can *Tommie* be here?" There wasn't a second to spare to tell him anything.

"Let me tell her good-bye," JimDaddy said.

"I did," Paulie said. "I let her say good-bye that day."

Then he looked at me.

"That was it," I said, knowing. "When she said her farewells."

For a moment I saw Tommie move toward her father as he ran up on the car crash. That terrible accident. All the sirens. The wailing. People standing nearby. Some crying. Others filming. There was Paulie, leaning in the window of the crushed car. And Tommie easing over to her father and whispering in his ear as the sun disappeared in a flash of light as tiny and bright as a firefly.

I could see Buddy in the backseat. Opening the car door. Climbing out. Not a scratch on him.

"Tommie slipped away then," I said.

113

There wasn't a lot of mumbo jumbo when me and Paulie held Tommie's hands and walked her outside to where her mother waited on the lawn. I might have been able to do that all along. If I had known how.

"Good-bye, Evie," she said. "Tell my daddy I love him. He doesn't need me anymore. I can go on." She smiled. "Thank you."

I swallowed at a hedgehog lodged in my throat. "I'll miss you."

"Don't you worry," she said. "I'll be waiting for you when you come on over."

Uh.

Then she was gone.

"For good?" I asked Paulie.

He nodded. "Just needed someone this side of the veil," he said, "who loved her to show the way. That's all. Pointing them to the light."

And from the porch Aunt Odie said, "Makes sense."

I stood in the yard, the sky so clear I could see every star.

"Helping her go will ease up some of this grief," Paulie said. "It stayed so heavy 'cause she got caught."

"What about those people at your place?" I asked Paulie.

"What people?" Aunt Odie asked.

"I'll tell you later," I said.

"Different clientele," Paulie said. "They're not stuck. Just want to help those left behind."

I nodded. Stared at the sky again.

When we walked back into the house, everyone looked at us, wide-eyed.

"Where's my daughter?" JimDaddy asked.

"She's gone on," I said.

Momma stood. Took a deep breath. "They're both right here," she said, gesturing at me and Baby Lucy. JimDaddy nodded, pulled me into a hug. Momma handed him Baby Lucy, who laughed and pointed at the ceiling as he held her.

114

I stood on the porch with Buddy. His momma had found him
missing from his place and called him eight times. Now she
stood across the street, staring at us, hands on her hips.

"Come to the swing," he said. "The light will go out."

We walked across the front porch. The smell of petunias
floated in the air.

"I see those that passed on," I said. "It's a Messenger Gift.
You just as well know."

"I'm glad you told me."

The light clicked off.

"May I kiss you good night, Evie Messenger?"

I answered by kissing him first.

"What's your name?"

The girl tilts her head and her hair floats to her shoulders, like a butterfly ready to land.

"I can't remember," she says.

I blink in the dark.

The room is comfortable. I'm comfortable. Even though I'm getting ready to start this all again, it feels right.

"What do you remember?"

She's quiet. In slow motion she becomes more real, more there.

"I just know everyone loved me."

I nod. "Okay," I say.

She's close enough to touch now. I feel her in the air around me. Feel she was loved.

"Maybe I can help."